For Alex and Juliet

HIGHBURY HOUSE

School for the Daughters of Gentlefolk

GROUND FLOOR

KITCHEN GARDEN

SCULLERY

KITCHEN

CORRIDOR

REFECTORY / DINING ROOM

STORE ROOM

COURTYARD

CLASSROOM

CLASSROOMS

MISS DE VERE'S SITTING ROOM

ELLY Griffiths

A GIRL CALLED JUSTICE

Quercus

QUERCUS CHILDREN'S BOOKS

First published in Great Britain in 2019
by Hodder and Stoughton

1 3 5 7 9 10 8 6 4 2

A CIP catalogue record for this book
is available from the British Library.

ISBN 978 1 786 54059 1

Printed and bound by CPI Group (UK) Ltd, Croydon, CR0 4YY

The paper and board used in this book
are made from wood from responsible sources.

Quercus Children's Books
An imprint of
Hachette Children's Group
Part of Hodder and Stoughton
Carmelite House
50 Victoria Embankment
London EC4Y 0DZ
An Hachette UK Company
www.hachette.co.uk
www.hachettechildrens.co.uk

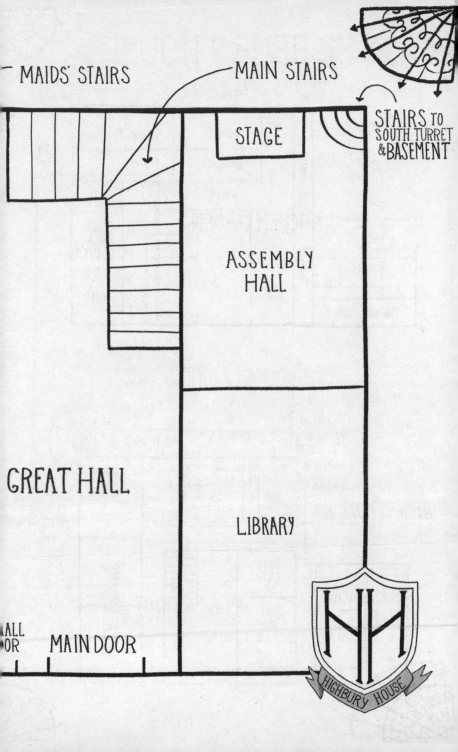

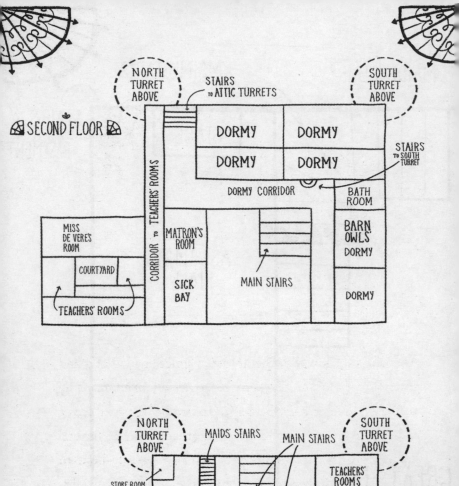

SECOND FLOOR

NORTH TURRET ABOVE

STAIRS TO ATTIC TURRETS

SOUTH TURRET ABOVE

DORMY

DORMY

DORMY

DORMY

STAIRS TO SOUTH TURRET

CORRIDOR TO TEACHERS' ROOMS

DORMY CORRIDOR

BATH ROOM

MISS DE VERE'S ROOM

MATRON'S ROOM

MAIN STAIRS

BARN OWLS' DORMY

COURTYARD

SICK BAY

DORMY

TEACHERS' ROOMS

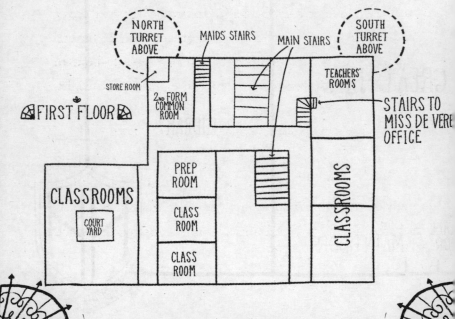

FIRST FLOOR

NORTH TURRET ABOVE

MAIDS' STAIRS

MAIN STAIRS

SOUTH TURRET ABOVE

STORE ROOM

2ND FORM COMMON ROOM

TEACHERS' ROOMS

STAIRS TO MISS DE VERE OFFICE

CLASSROOMS

PREP ROOM

CLASS ROOM

CLASS ROOM

COURT YARD

CLASSROOMS

CHAPTER 1

9th October 1936

As soon as she saw the school, Justice Jones knew that it had potential for murder. She kept this to herself, of course. The taxi driver could easily be a spy. To be fair, the taxi driver hadn't said much beyond a sort of groan when he heaved Justice's trunk into the boot, but Justice wasn't about to accept silence as a proof of innocence. As Leslie Light, private investigator, always said: *it's what your suspect doesn't say. That's what you have to listen to.*

You could see the school from miles away, a looming black shape with towers at each corner. It looked as if it was built by someone who wanted to make a point: School is Serious, School is Not Fun, School is actually very much like Prison. Justice stared it down, daring it to intimidate her.

The building only looks so big, she thought, *because the land around it is so flat*. The Romney Marshes, that's what it said on the map, but all Justice could see were endless fields of grey – featureless and almost colourless – merging seamlessly with the sky. Presumably the sea was there somewhere but she couldn't see it, though she could hear the seagulls high above, calling in wind-blown desolate voices. It was a good thing that she wasn't easily spooked, Justice told herself, because if ever a place was too spooky for its own good, it was Highbury House Boarding School for the Daughters of Gentlefolk.

Getting out her journal, Justice wrote:

FIRST THOUGHTS ON HIGHBURY HOUSE
Resembles: Dracula's castle and/or a prison
Surrounding land: extremely flat. Much like my mood.
Only one local taxi firm: Nye and Son. Assume I'm being driven by
    Nye and not by Son as he's about 100. And possibly a spy.
Chance of escaping school without being seen: minimal.
Also, potential for murder: high.

'Nearly there,' said Nye suddenly.

Justice looked at her watch. It was only five o'clock but already it was nearly night. That's what you got for starting a new school in October, of course.

'What's Highbury House like?' she asked, spotting a chance to get some background information from a valuable local source. 'I've never been to boarding school before.'

Actually, she had never been to any sort of school.

Nye was silent for a few seconds, chewing on his long grey moustache. Then he said, 'I don't see school folk much. My brother drove out here last week though.'

'Really?' said Justice. 'Is he a taxi driver too?'

'No,' said Nye, swerving to avoid a low-flying heron. 'He's the local undertaker.'

'Undertaker?' said Justice. 'Did someone die?'

But Nye did not answer and the rest of the drive passed in silence.

Justice watched as the looming towers came closer and closer. The sky darkened and a baleful moon appeared behind the clouds. Nye stopped and got out of the car to open heavy iron gates, a stone griffin on each side. He had a key, Justice noted. *What sort of a school keeps its pupils locked in?*

The sign on the gates was still just legible in the gloom.

Highbury House Boarding School for the Daughters of Gentlefolk

What *were* gentlefolk anyway? Justice had a premonition that none of the inhabitants of the grey stone mansion would prove particularly gentle.

Nye drove through the gates and on down the driveway. It seemed to go on for ever. Justice could see pitches of some kind (she was vague on all sports), outhouses and a greenhouse. Then they were pulling up in front of huge oak double doors. Nye got out surprisingly quickly for someone so ancient, heaved Justice's trunk out of the boot and muttered something that could have been 'Goodbye' or even, 'Good luck.' And then he was driving away, leaving Justice standing in front of the locked and bolted doors.

Was she supposed to knock, or what? As she waited, her breath misting in the cold, a dark bird – or was it a bat? – circled one of the towers. She wanted to turn and run but Nye was nowhere to be seen and, besides, where would she go? *Screw your courage to the sticking place*, her mother used to say. Justice was never quite sure what it meant but it was a quote from *Macbeth* and she seemed to remember that the play didn't end too happily.

Justice was still standing there, uncertain, when a smaller door within the big door creaked open. A tiny, but nonetheless menacing, silhouette was framed in the doorway.

'Are you Joan?' said the figure.

'No,' said Justice.

The woman, who Justice now saw was wearing a nurse's uniform, consulted a list. 'It says here, Joan Justice. New Girl.'

'My name's Justice,' said Justice. 'Justice Jones.'

'Oh.' The woman seemed annoyed. 'We assumed that must be a mistake. We've got you down as Joan.'

'Maybe you are thinking of my surname – Jones. My first name's Justice,' said Justice. 'My father's a barrister.'

'We know *that*,' said the woman. 'Herbert Jones QC. He's quite famous, isn't he?'

'He's defended a lot of murderers,' said Justice.

The woman gave her a very hard look as if suspecting her of cheek. 'I'm Matron,' she said, smiling suddenly and showing lots of orange gum. 'Hutchins here will take your trunk.'

As she spoke a man appeared around the side of the house. He looked about nine feet tall, with broad shoulders and a disconcertingly small head. The glance he gave Justice might have been unfriendly, or it might even have been pitying – it was hard to tell. Justice tried a tentative smile which was not returned. Hutchins picked up her trunk with one hand and lumbered away with it.

'Come in, Justice,' said Matron, managing to convey the impression that Justice had been keeping her waiting. 'Hutchins will be locking up soon.'

And, clutching her overnight case and lacrosse stick, Justice stepped over the threshold of Highbury House.

She found herself in a massive hall, panelled and echoey. A wide staircase led upwards, past gloomy oil paintings of people who looked as if they had been dead for ever. A suit of armour stood to attention beside a stone fireplace containing only an unlit log. Justice shivered involuntarily. It was as cold inside as out.

'I've asked Eva to look after you,' said Matron. 'She's in the second-form common room.'

That meant that Eva was Justice's age. Twelve. Or maybe Eva was already thirteen? Justice had been told that she would be in the second form and had been pleased that at least she wouldn't be the youngest in the school. There were eight forms at Highbury House, from the first form to the upper sixth and including something inexplicably called 'the remove'. 'I look forward to meeting her,' Justice said.

Matron looked positively appalled at this presumption. Clearly it was a mistake to have said anything. 'Do you have your health certificate?'

Justice reached into her bag and handed it over. 'Good. Follow me,' said Matron.

Justice tried to map the route in her head but it was impossible. Through several doors, across a small courtyard (the plants grey and windswept), through what was obviously a dining hall, up a stone staircase, along a panelled corridor and eventually into a small room with window seats and faded sofas. Eva was sitting expectantly on one of the seats.

'Eva, this is Justice,' said Matron. 'Not Joan, Justice.'

'Golly,' said Eva, eyes wide.

Eva was a small, sandy-haired girl. She was dressed in a brown blazer with gold trim. Under this she had a brown skirt, yellow-and-white striped shirt and long brown socks. But Justice did not think that she was actually insane; this was the school uniform. Justice had hers in her bag but she hadn't dared try it on yet.

'Eva will show you to your dormy,' said Matron. 'Meal is at six. Goodbye, girls.'

7

That smile again.

'What's *Meal*?' said Justice when Matron had gone.

'It's what we eat in the evening,' said Eva. 'Dead baby mostly.'

'Dead baby?'

'It's a sort of pudding,' said Eva. 'You're in my dormy. Barnowls. We're all super friends. Shall I show you the way?'

'Please,' said Justice, picking up her overnight bag. She felt slightly bewildered by so many new words at once. Barnowls. Dormy. Dead baby. What did it all *mean*?

On the way, Eva told Justice that she was twelve and had been at Highbury House for a year and at the prep school before that. Her best friend was Nora and they both worshipped Helena Bliss, the head girl.

'What do your people do?' Eva asked as they climbed another stone staircase.

'My people?'

'Your mater and pater.'

Justice blinked. This was Latin, she knew, but she'd never heard anyone her age *speak* Latin in normal life before. Though to be fair, she'd never heard anyone her age speak much of anything before. She supposed this was how everyone spoke here. 'My father's a lawyer, my mother's dead.'

'Dead?' Eva's eyes grew round. 'How ghastly.'

'Well, it was a little while ago,' said Justice. Actually, it was exactly thirty-one days ago, but she didn't like to say this out loud. For one thing, saying it aloud made it real and, for another, people being sympathetic made her want to cry and, if there was one thing she wasn't going to do at Highbury House, it was cry. 'My mother used to teach me at home,' she said, changing the subject. 'I've never been to school before.'

'Oh, poor you.' Eva squeezed her arm but then, mercifully, let go. 'You'll love it here. It's super.'

More corridors, more odd little staircases. *Always know where your nearest exit is.* That's what Leslie Light said in *The Case of the Haunted Hotel.* But Justice was completely lost in this strange, rambling building. Still, here was a chance to solve her own mystery.

'Eva,' said Justice, catching up with her guide, 'Mr Nye, the taxi driver, said someone had died here recently. Do you know anything about that?'

Eva turned. Her face had changed in some way but Justice wasn't quite sure how.

'That was Mary,' she whispered. 'She was a servant. Miss de Vere said we weren't to talk about it.' Eva stopped beside a door half concealed by panelling.

'Here's our dormy. Isn't it super?' she said, throwing open the door.

Justice looked at the long room. There were five beds, divided by white-painted partitions. The windows were small and high up. The only light came from a single bulb at the far end of the room.

Eva was looking at Justice, clearly expecting a response. 'Super,' said Justice.

When Eva went to the bathroom, leaving her in the dormy to get changed, Justice updated her journal:

FIRST THOUGHTS ON HIGHBURY HOUSE
Resembles: Dracula's castle and/or a prison
Surrounding land: extremely flat. Much like my mood.
Only one local taxi firm: Nye and Son. Assume I'm being driven by
    Nye and not by Son as he's about 100. And possibly a spy.
Chance of escaping school without being seen: minimal.
Also, potential for murder: high.

THOUGHTS ON HIGHBURY HOUSE cont'd
Nye: brother of the undertaker. Knows more than he's letting on?
Matron: eyes don't change when she smiles. Has heard of Dad
    (suspicious?).

Hutchins: strong, will know secrets of the house.
Eva: small, stupid. Was scared when I mentioned Mary.
Mary: query, murdered?

CHAPTER 2

Matron had told Justice to change into her school uniform so she supposed she'd better get on with it. The only way she could force herself to put on the brown socks was to pretend that she was a Yankee in the American Civil War going undercover as a Confederate soldier. She remembered what her mum always said about uniforms: *Dress people the same and they'll start to think the same and that's dangerous.*

But you're not here now, Mum, Justice told her silently, *and I've got to be a schoolgirl for a bit.*

Eva came back to take her to Meal and obviously to check that she'd dressed herself properly.

'Oh, you do look nice,' she said. 'Just like a regular schoolgirl.'

'Um, thanks?' said Justice.

'I like your hair,' said Eva. 'It's very pretty.'

'Thanks,' said Justice again, slightly surprised. Her hair was short and dark and she'd tucked it neatly behind her ears. She'd never thought about whether it was pretty or not. Her mother had brought her up not to think about her looks and she didn't really have any girlfriends. Her best (and only) friend, Peter, was currently at a music school in London and, although she and Peter had discussed every subject under the sun, they were not in the habit of discussing hairstyles.

Eva led Justice down two flights of stairs and back across the courtyard again. It was completely dark outside now and as they crossed the courtyard Justice looked up to see the black shapes which could be bats swooping around one of the towers. She remembered seeing the towers – turrets, Eva had called them – from the driveway. *Was this the North Turret?* thought Justice, trying to get her bearings. She thought that they might go through the grand entrance hall but Eva seemed to be sticking to stone corridors with low ceilings – no panels, no suits of armour. Eventually they arrived at a pair of double doors. Eva flung them open with a flourish. 'The dining hall,' she said.

14

The first thing that struck Justice was the noise. It was deafening. Chairs scraping against the tiled floor, knives and forks rattling, voices raised to such a pitch that Justice thought the bats must be getting pretty good reception. Rows and rows and rows of girls were sitting at long tables, and almost every head seemed, for that second, to be turned towards them . . . before returning to whatever they'd been doing before. Eva took Justice's arm. 'We're late. We need to get our food.' They collected their trays and then went to a hatch where a woman in a blue apron slopped something unspeakable on to their plates.

'You can have as much bread as you want,' said Eva, putting three solid white slices on to her tray.

'I'm all right, thanks,' said Justice. She'd been starving in the taxi but now, suddenly, her appetite had disappeared.

Eva then led her to the end of one of the tables.

'Barnies,' she said, sounding like a circus ringmaster, 'this is Justice.'

Three pairs of eyes – two blue, one brown – turned in her direction.

'I thought she was called Joan,' said a girl with long blonde hair in plaits.

'Yes, sorry,' said Eva. *Sorry?* 'She's called Justice Jones.'

'What sort of a name's that?' said Blonde Plaits.

15

'My father's a lawyer,' said Justice, to remind them she wasn't invisible. 'What's your name?'

Like Matron earlier, the girl's expression seemed to imply that Justice should not have spoken. After a bit of plait tossing, she said, 'I'm Rose. Rose Trevellian-Hayes.'

'I'm Nora,' volunteered a tall girl with glasses. She gave Justice a little grin which, like her glasses, was slightly askew.

'I'm Stella,' said the third girl. Stella's brown eyes met Justice's and she gave her a rather grave smile.

'Your hair's very short,' said Rose in what sounded like a slightly accusatory tone.

There seemed no answer to this, so Justice didn't offer one. She tried to eat a bit of the food in front of her and put her spoon down hastily.

'You won't be able to keep it tied back like us,' said Rose. 'I've got the longest hair at Highbury House,' she added.

Eva's hair was obviously longer, but nobody mentioned this.

'Rose has got hair like an angel,' said Eva.

'Actually, angels are mostly men, I think,' said Justice, then after no one said anything, 'You know, Michael and Gabriel and so on. And Lucifer, of course.'

The four Barnowls stared at her.

'Where did you go to school before?' asked Rose, narrowing her eyes.

'My mother taught me at home,' said Justice. 'But she died so my father sent me here.'

'That's awful,' said Nora. 'How did she die?'

Justice had steeled herself for questions about her mother and had planned to answer them in a calm, factual voice but, when faced with four curious and sympathetic faces, it was harder than she had thought it would be.

'She had cancer,' said Justice.

'I'm sorry,' said Stella. And she sounded like she really was. There was a silence and then Stella said, 'It must be nice to be taught at home.'

Justice was grateful to her for changing the subject, but she didn't want to talk about being at home with Mum, not when she was trying so hard not to show her real feelings.

'You might find the work here quite hard though,' said Rose in a voice that seemed to be trying hard to sound sympathetic and failing spectacularly.

'Maybe not,' said Nora. 'She could be a genius.'

'Nora's a brain,' said Eva.

'Oh, I'm not,' said Nora, pushing her glasses further up her nose.

'How many girls are in our form?' asked Justice.

'Fifteen,' said Rose, pushing her plate away untouched. 'Us five Barnowls, five Doves and five Robins.'

'Nora came third in the form last year,' said Eva. 'I came fourteenth.'

'Who came top?'

'Stella.'

In that case, Stella's the brain, thought Justice. But she soon came to realise that because Nora wore glasses, she was automatically 'a brain', just as Rose being blonde and pretty meant she must have the longest hair. She wasn't surprised that Eva had come fourteenth and she betted that Rose was exactly in the middle. She made mental notes of all this so she could jot it down later.

'Alicia came second,' said Rose. 'She could have come first if she'd wanted to.'

'Alicia is Rose's best friend,' said Eva. 'She's in Doves and because we had a spare place Rose was hoping . . .'

Rose was hoping she'd move to Barnowls, thought Justice, *but instead they've got me*. It wasn't a promising start as far as being 'super friends' went.

Eva looked like she was about to say more but, just as she was about to speak, a stupefying change came over the girls at the table. They all looked up with identical expressions of awe – mouths slightly open, eyes shining. It took Justice a few moments before she identified the cause of this chain reaction. A tall girl with long, wavy blonde hair had stopped at their table. What's more, the vision seemed to be addressing her, Justice.

'You must be the new girl,' it was saying. 'Welcome to Highbury House. I'm Helena Bliss, the head girl.'

'How do you do,' said Justice.

For some reason Helena laughed at this. 'That's right. Don't be afraid to speak up for yourself. It's Joan, isn't it?'

'Justice.'

'Oh.' Helena gave her a look as if suspecting insubordination but obviously decided not to take it further. 'Well, you're in good hands with the Barnowls. Look after her, girls. Remember, every time we meet a stranger we could be entertaining angels unaware.'

'We will, Helena.'

'You can rely on us, Helena.'

'Of course, Helena.'

'Thank you, Helena.'

The vision drifted away, leaving the Barnowls to ruffle their feathers excitedly.

'Isn't she beautiful?'

'She was wearing scent – did you smell it?'

'She actually said Justice was in good hands with us.'

'Why doesn't she have her hair tied up?' asked Justice.

The others stared at her.

'She's head girl.'

'She's Helena Bliss.'

'Her hair's just like yours, Rose,' said Eva. 'When you're head girl you can wear yours loose.'

'I can't wait,' said Rose, obviously not doubting for a minute that the day would come.

'Have you finished, Justice?' said Eva. 'We can leave the room if the prefects have left.'

'And don't worry,' said Stella, looking at Justice's plate, which was still full of uneaten food, 'we've got tuck in the dormy.'

'Tuck' turned out to be food, and the evening was not quite as bad as Justice had dreaded. They played ping-pong in the common room and Justice got to meet Alicia, Rose's best friend, who had white-blonde hair and pale eyes. The two of them immediately disappeared into the corner and carried on an intense, whispered conversation. Were they talking about her? Maybe, but Justice was too busy trying to hit the ball back to pay much attention.

At eight o'clock they retired to the dormy where Stella and Nora shared out fruit cake and slightly stale biscuits.

They sat on the floor to eat because 'Matron goes mad if she finds crumbs'.

'We take it in turns to share the food from our tuck boxes,' said Eva. 'Have you got a tuck box, Justice?'

'I don't think so. I could ask Dad to send something, I suppose.'

This met with an enthusiastic response. 'Yes, do!' said Nora. 'Tell him a good rich fruit cake because that doesn't go off.'

'Stuff in tins is good too,' added Stella. 'Sardines, pineapple chunks, that sort of thing.'

Justice tried and failed to imagine her father assembling a box of this sort of food. Maybe he'd ask his secretary to do it.

Rose, the dormy captain, was responsible for turning the lights off at nine. First there was a visit to the bathroom, an incredibly grim room that was the coldest place Justice had encountered so far. Then Rose ordered Eva and Nora to clear up and told Justice and Stella to close the curtains. As Justice went to the far window, she noticed something in the distance, a dark shape that seemed to be glimmering slightly in the darkness. What was it?

'What are you staring at, Justice?' said Rose. 'You should be in bed by now.'

'There's something out there. A light in some sort of building.'

'Oh, that's just the haunted tower,' said Eva.

'The haunted tower?'

'Lights out now,' barked Rose from the doorway, one hand on the switch.

'But you can read with a torch under the covers,' said Stella to Justice as they jumped into their beds, 'as long as Matron doesn't catch you.'

'Maybe Justice doesn't have a torch,' said Rose.

But she did. Her mother used to say: *There are three things you'll always need: a torch, a penknife and a compass.* So when Justice knew that she had to go to boarding school, she had prepared her own 'survival kit'. She added a journal and pen which her mother would certainly have done too, because she was author. She wrote the Leslie Light books, about a Classics professor who was also a private investigator. They were really good mysteries because you were never sure who did it until the last page. And now Justice suspected that she had wandered into her very own crime novel. By the trusty yellow light of her pocket torch, Justice wrote:

HIGHBURY HOUSE:
It's every bit as bad as I expected. Perhaps even worse?
Conditions: squalid.
Food: inedible.

Company: mixed.
The girls aren't that bad though Rose has potential to be a
*   psychopath. Stella seems nice and Eva is harmless enough. Nora is*
*   considered clever, though I think Stella is cleverer. Possible ally?*

TO INVESTIGATE:
Mary's mysterious death
Helena Bliss: Rose lookalike. Has a strange hold over the others.
The Haunted Tower: ???

Justice switched off her torch. She slipped her journal under her pillow. She'd have to find a better hiding place for it tomorrow. The room was dark, full of the sounds of heavy breathing and the occasional squeak that seemed to be coming from Eva. There was still a faint light though, a silvery streak filtering through from the high window at the end of the room. Was it moonlight or a candle in the window of the haunted tower? Justice imagined herself flying out of the dormy window, circling the house and the tower and winging her way across the marshes towards the sea. But where would she go? That was the trouble. She couldn't go home because Dad didn't want her there and Mum . . . well, she wouldn't be there, would she?

So Justice had to stay where she was. For now, at least. Till she could persuade her dad to let her come home. But for now ... Justice sighed and tried to find a comfortable spot on her pillow. 'I made it through the first day, Mum,' she whispered into the darkness.

CHAPTER 3

Justice's first thought was that the building must be on fire. Why else would a bell be ringing in the middle of the night? But even as she groped for her torch, she heard a voice in her ear saying,

'Wake up, Justice. It's morning.'

Morning? The sky, what she could see of it through a gap in the curtains, was still pitch black. Sitting up and rubbing her eyes she saw Stella smiling at her from the end of the bed.

'It's seven o'clock,' she said. 'We need to be at breakfast by half past. Lessons start at half past eight.'

Half past *eight*? At home Justice often didn't get up until nine. One of her mum's theories was that young people needed their sleep. They would have breakfast at ten – in the summer they would have it in the garden under the lime tree that dropped sticky resin on the table – and start their lessons at eleven. To her horror, Justice realised that she was nearly crying. She turned away from Stella, rubbing her eyes again.

'Are you all right?' said Stella softly.

'Yes, fine,' said Justice. 'Where's the bathroom? I'll have to have my bath quickly.'

Rose, passing by in pink-patterned pyjamas, burst out laughing. 'Did you hear that, Barnies? Justice wants a bath.'

'What's wrong with that?' said Justice. 'I have a bath every day.'

'You must be very dirty then,' said Rose. 'Here you have a bath once a week. In the mornings you just have to wash your face and under your arms. I go first because I'm dormy captain.' And she swept out of the room, carrying her toothbrush and towel.

A rather awkward silence followed. 'You can go next, Justice,' said Eva. 'I hate washing in the mornings. It's so cold in the bathroom.'

'Sometimes there are icicles on the inside of the windows,' said Stella. 'Matron thinks it's healthy to have the windows open, you see.'

'Fresh air, girls!' said Nora in a voice which was clearly intended to impersonate Matron. Unfortunately, at that moment, the real thing appeared in the doorway.

Matron was a small woman, not much taller than Justice, but she somehow seemed to make herself look like a giant. She loomed over the suddenly silent girls.

'What was that, Nora?'

'Nothing, Matron.'

'I hope you're all putting your best feet forward. Beds need to be made, hair brushed and tied back.' Her eyes gleamed with something like manic fervour. Or it could be cataracts – Justice wasn't sure.

When Matron left, Eva burst into giggles, and soon Stella and Nora, and even Justice, couldn't help but join in. It felt good to laugh, thought Justice, though the laughter ended abruptly when Rose came back into the room, at which point Justice made good her escape to the bathroom.

Stella was right – the bathroom was freezing. It was also even more awful in the daylight: cracked tiles, paint peeling from the ceiling, green mould taking over the bath and sink. Justice brushed her teeth and made a monster face in the age-spotted mirror. 'You can survive this,' she said out loud. Her voice echoed against the tiles and her breath billowed around her.

Back in the dormy she made her bed, copying how the other Barnowls did it. Last night she'd noticed a loose floorboard under the bed and now, surreptitiously, she knelt down, lifted the board and slipped her journal in the space underneath. Then she straightened up and crossed the room to look out of the high window at the far end. Dawn was breaking over the marshes but there was still mist on the ground; it gave Justice a strange topsy-turvy feeling, as if she was looking down from above the clouds. She remembered the odd glimmering light from last night and craned her head round until she could see the tower standing on its own about two hundred yards away, absurdly sinister in the grey dawn.

'Why's the tower haunted?' she asked, looking back at the girls in the room.

She didn't believe in ghosts herself, but she was sure that Highbury House simply teemed with charming stories about headless spectres, clanking chains and mysterious grey ladies. She looked again at the tower. Maybe it was a trick of the light but, all of a sudden, she seemed to see a glint in one of the narrow windows, as if someone was holding a mirror up to the sun.

Eva gave one of her squeaks. 'Oh, it's such a spooky story. A girl died there, years ago, and you can still hear her crying at night sometimes. You tell it, Nora. You're the best at ghost stories.'

Nora adjusted her glasses and looked ready to start but Rose interjected.

'We haven't got time for that now. Hurry up or we'll be late for breakfast.'

Breakfast was porridge, grey and unappetising. But Justice was starving and she managed to eat it all. At least there was toast too, and even the Highbury House cook couldn't entirely ruin toast. The girls weren't allowed to start eating until Helena Bliss had stood up and said Grace. '*Benedictus benedicat.*'

'That's Latin,' said Eva. 'Do you know any Latin, Justice? It's my worst subject.'

'My mother taught me a bit,' said Justice. Mum had studied Classics at Oxford before the war, though she wasn't allowed to take any exams because she was a woman. Justice didn't want to talk about her mother, so she tried another topic of conversation.

'How come you're all at Highbury House?' she asked the table in general. She had been thinking about this in the night. Why would any parent choose to send their daughter to an isolated school on the edge of Romney Marsh?

'Mummy came here,' said Rose as if this explained everything. 'Miss de Vere was the English teacher then. She'd just started teaching.' Miss de Vere was the headmistress, her name in prim gold letters on the sign by the gates.

'My mother came here too,' said Eva. 'My people are abroad so I've been here since Infants.'

'Highbury House is very exclusive,' said Rose. 'And extremely expensive.'

'I'm on a scholarship,' Stella told Justice. 'My parents haven't got any money.'

'That's nothing to be proud of,' said Rose.

'Well, it is, because it means that Stella's very clever,' said Justice, and was surprised to receive a grateful smile from Stella.

Rose tossed her hair. 'Why are you here, Justice?'

'My father knows Miss de Vere,' said Justice. She wasn't entirely sure how or why her father knew the headmistress, but she wasn't going to admit this.

Rose looked as if she was about to say more but she stopped because a figure in a maid's uniform was approaching their table.

'Look out,' she drawled, 'it's Dotty Dorothy.'

The maid, a girl who didn't look much older than Justice, stopped at their table. 'Please, I'm to take Miss Jones to see Miss de Vere.'

'There she is.' Rose made a lordly gesture in Justice's direction.

'Good luck, Justice,' whispered Stella as she got up.

As Justice followed Dorothy out of the room, watched by four hundred curious eyes, she wondered: *Why on earth would I need luck?*

CHAPTER 4

Miss de Vere's office was at the top of the South Turret. *A handy way to make the headmistress seem superior*, thought Justice. According to the Barnowls, the rooms at the top of the other three turrets were locked, 'because otherwise you can get out on to the roof'. Justice tried to remember the geography of the building: the kitchens, dining room, assembly hall, library and great hall were all on the ground floor, the classrooms on the first floor, and the dormitories on the second. But Dorothy seemed to be taking a very strange route, along endless corridors and up twisting flights of stairs.

'Hang on,' said Justice as Dorothy whisked around a corner. She wanted to talk to her – she could be an important witness in the mystery of what happened to the other servant girl. 'What's the hurry?'

Dorothy turned. She had a little, pointed face with anxious eyes and mousy hair scraped back into a bun.

'Miss de Vere said at once,' whispered Dorothy and she set off again, almost trotting now.

Justice caught her up. 'What's Miss de Vere like?' she asked.

Dorothy looked over her shoulder. 'She's the headmistress,' she said, as if this answered the question. Which perhaps it did.

'I was sorry to hear about Mary,' said Justice as innocently as she could. 'Was she a friend of yours?'

Now Dorothy did stop. She stopped and stared at Justice, eyes huge, pupils dilated. 'I didn't have anything to do with it.'

'With what?'

'Dorothy!' A voice that seemed to have been shot from a cannon. A large woman carrying a lacrosse stick was marching along the corridor.

'What are you doing, standing here and chatting? Haven't you got work to do?'

'Please, Miss Thomas, I'm taking the new girl to see Miss de Vere.'

'Well, take her then, and don't stand around chatting. And you – new girl – we don't gossip to servants in this school. Understood?'

'I think so,' said Justice. She was trying to be honest, but Miss Thomas gave her a hard stare.

'Cut along then.'

They cut along. Justice wanted to ask more but Dorothy was scurrying in front of her with her head down, obviously too terrified to speak. She led Justice along corridors lined with stuffed animal heads and more of those gloomy oil paintings. Justice had already noticed that the school was divided into pupil areas (stone floors, dim lighting, peeling paintwork) and parts that were reserved for the staff only (carpets, velvet curtains, the occasional dusty-looking chandelier). This was definitely a staff-only area. Dorothy stopped by one of the doors.

'It's up there,' she said.

'Up?' said Justice, turning the door handle. But when she turned back Dorothy had gone.

Justice pushed open the door and saw a small spiral staircase in front of her. She climbed the narrow stairs, which were covered in a thick red carpet, and reached a door with a plaque saying 'Headmistress'. Justice stood there for a second, her heart beating so quickly that she could feel it thumping in her chest. Why was she so scared? Was it Stella's whispered 'good luck'? Was it the loud-voiced Miss Thomas? Was it because Dorothy was obviously frightened of something, something in this house? But she was letting the atmosphere get to her – a classic mistake. Again, she heard her mother's voice saying, *Screw your courage to the sticking place*, and steeling herself, she knocked loudly on the door.

Miss de Vere was younger than Justice had expected. She had imagined the headmistress as a white-haired figure, possibly leaning on an ebony cane. Instead Miss de Vere was dark and rather glamorous with white skin, blue eyes and hair in a fashionable shingled style. She wore a teacher's gown, of course, but underneath she had a green dress and what looked like rather good pearls. She also had a letter open on her desk. Justice recognised the writing at once.

'Sit down, Justice.' Her voice was low and musical, but, for all that, Justice guessed that Miss de Vere could easily be as commanding as the terrifying Miss Thomas.

'How are you finding Highbury House?'

Justice wasn't sure what to say. 'It's like something out of a horror story', would probably sound rather rude. What about, 'I'm pretty sure that someone was murdered here recently'? Instead she said, 'It's very nice.'

'It must be very different to what you are used to.'

'Yes,' said Justice.

'Yes, *Miss de Vere.*'

'Yes, Miss de Vere.'

'I'm delighted to meet you,' said Miss de Vere in a more friendly voice. 'I'm an admirer of Veronica Burton's books.'

'Mum?' said Justice in surprise. Her mother's books were written under her maiden name so that people wouldn't link them to Dad's work. She knew that the books were popular, but Justice had thought that a headmistress would somehow be above reading crime novels.

'Your mother was a fine writer,' Miss de Vere said.

'Yes, she was,' said Justice. She suddenly found that she had a lump in her throat. *Please don't say anything else about her*, she prayed silently.

Luckily Miss de Vere moved on to Dad. 'I've had a letter from your father. He says that you are very advanced academically. Ordinarily, when a girl has had little formal schooling, I put her in a form with slightly younger students but, in your case, I'm going to keep you in the second form.'

'Thank you,' said Justice, feeling that some remark was called for.

'And the Barnowls are a nice group of girls. Boarding school can be difficult,' Miss de Vere went on. 'Everyone cooped up together all the time, especially in an isolated place like this. Tensions can rise, tempers can flare unexpectedly, words get spoken that cannot easily be revoked. You need to have great inner strength to survive. I always tell my girls that it's useful to have a hobby, something that can occupy your mind and take you out of yourself. Do you have a hobby, Justice?'

'I like reading,' said Justice, not adding that she mostly read the Leslie Light novels and accounts of old murder trials. 'And I keep a journal.'

'Excellent. We have a fine library here and I encourage girls to read at least a book a week. Do you like Jane Austen, Justice?'

'I've only read *Pride and Prejudice*, but I enjoyed that.'

Miss de Vere reached around to the shelves behind her and took down a small, red-leather book. 'Try this one. I think you'll like it.'

Justice looked at the cover. *Northanger Abbey*. 'Thank you,' she said.

Miss de Vere smiled and handed Justice a typewritten sheet of paper. 'This is your timetable. You're in Latin with Miss Bathurst first lesson.'

'Thank you,' said Justice. Miss de Vere was obviously expecting her to go but Justice couldn't help herself. She took a deep breath and said, 'Miss de Vere, what did Mary die of?'

The headmistress's face didn't change and yet it was suddenly completely different. She was even still smiling but, now, the smile seemed the most terrifying thing that Justice had seen since arriving at Highbury House.

'Never end a sentence on a preposition,' she said. 'Now go to your lessons.'

CHAPTER 5

So Justice's life as a schoolgirl began. The Latin mistress Miss Bathurst was a chaotic figure with wispy grey hair that looked in constant danger of escaping from her bun. She shed hairpins as she walked about the class and the more helpful girls picked them up for her. Miss Bathurst gave Justice a page of Latin to translate into English ('Just give us an idea. Don't worry about making mistakes') and Justice was relieved that she was able to do it without too much trouble.

'Well!' said Miss Bathurst, looking up from Justice's paper with a rather twisted smile. 'We have a Latin scholar in our midst!'

Rose's friend Alicia looked thoroughly fed up.

'Why didn't you tell us you were so good at Latin?' said Nora when Miss Bathurst had hurried away in a flurry of dropped papers and escaping hairpins.

'I'm . . . I'm not really,' said Justice. 'My mum always liked it, I suppose.'

'Awful to have Latin as your best subject,' whispered Rose loudly to Alicia.

Maths was next. The teacher, Miss Morris, a weathered-looking woman with short hair and glasses, at least seemed fairly well-organised. She gave Justice a short written test and then moved her into a group with Stella, Alicia and an intense-looking girl called Irene. It was quite fun. They were working on equations and Miss Morris occasionally threw something more challenging into the mix. Using your brain, Justice realised, was one of the ways of forgetting that you were unhappy.

After maths it was time for something called recess. They trooped into the refectory where they were allowed a glass of barley water and one biscuit each, then they were sent out into the courtyard. The whole school seemed to be there and, again, the noise, bouncing off the stone walls, was almost unbearable. For a moment Justice just stood there, unable to move. She could feel her heart beating in double time again.

Was she about to have some kind of attack? Well, at least it would get her away from Highbury House.

She hadn't noticed that Stella was by her side until she felt a hand on her arm.

'Are you all right, Justice?'

'Yes,' said Justice, although she was finding it hard to speak. 'Just a bit . . . cold.' Which wasn't a lie. It was absolutely freezing in the courtyard.

'Let's go and sit on the radiator in the corridor,' said Stella. 'We're not allowed to but the teachers never come down in recess. They've got a proper fire in their common room. The beasts.'

The radiator was only lukewarm, but it felt like heaven after the courtyard. Stella and Justice squeezed themselves on to it. Through the window Justice could see out into the courtyard. Eva and Nora were doing something called 'recess duty' which seemed to involve making sure no one had a second biscuit. Rose and Alicia could be seen in a corner, talking intently.

'I'll bet this all seems really strange to you,' said Stella.

'It is a bit odd,' said Justice carefully. 'I was used to it being just me and my mum, you see.'

'It must be hard,' said Stella. Something in her voice made Justice feel comforted. It wasn't just sympathy; it was as if Stella really understood. She began to feel warm again, and not just from the radiator.

'I've got four brothers and two sisters,' said Stella. 'You never have any time for yourself. I used to long to be an only child.'

Justice was grateful that Stella hadn't asked any questions about her mother. 'I always wanted brothers and sisters,' she said. 'I suppose you always want what you haven't got.'

'That sounds like one of Miss de Vere's assemblies,' said Stella. 'They've always got a moral at the end. "Do unto others", that sort of thing.'

'What's Miss de Vere like?' asked Justice.

'She's all right,' said Stella. 'She can be quite scary though. Really nice one minute and then cold as ice.'

Justice thought of the way Miss de Vere's face had changed when she mentioned Mary.

'Everything's cold in this school,' she said.

Stella laughed. 'You're right. I don't think my feet have been warm once since I've been here.' There was a short, companionable silence and then she said, 'Which book did Miss de Vere give you?'

'*Northanger Abbey*,' said Justice. 'Why?'

'It's a kind of test. Miss de Vere believes that Jane Austen teaches you about life. I got *Persuasion*.'

It was rather disappointing that everyone was given a book. Justice couldn't remember what *Northanger Abbey* was about but, if it was anything like *Pride and Prejudice*, the headmistress seemed to be implying that she'd better marry a rich man as soon as possible. And Justice wasn't marrying anyone. Not even Peter.

'Do you like it here?' asked Justice. It didn't seem possible, but presumably some of the girls enjoyed their life at Highbury House.

Stella shrugged. 'It's all right. It's meant to be a good school. My parents were glad when I got a scholarship. I wish it was nearer home though. It feels miles from anywhere in the winter.'

'Where do your family live?'

'London,' said Stella. 'Parents can come down on the half-term holiday but mine can't afford it. I won't see them until the hols.'

'The holidays seem ages away,' said Justice. She was marking the days in her journal. She wondered if Dad would come to see her on the half holiday. Probably he'd be too busy.

Stella's eyes were kind. 'It's not so bad. We have fun sometimes and it's lovely in the spring. The marsh is covered in flowers.'

Her first morning at school seemed to have lasted for ever, thought Justice as the bell rang for the next lesson. Spring was a lifetime away.

Her timetable for the afternoon said 'GAMES' in ominous capitals. But it started to rain during lunch, hail battering against the windows, so Justice assumed that games would be cancelled. *Maybe*, she thought, *she could even spend the afternoon investigating Mary's mysterious death. Someone in the school must know* something.

Stella laughed bitterly when Justice expressed her hope that games might be cancelled.

'You must be joking. We have to have games even if it's *snowing*. There's a rumour that Miss Thomas once lost a girl when a fog came down during a cross-country run.'

'How can you lose one of your own pupils?' said Justice.

'Have you met Miss Thomas?' said Stella.

'Briefly.'

'There you are then. All she cares about is winning lacrosse matches.'

It was still raining when Justice entered the changing room with its wooden benches and rows of hooks. This room was even colder than the rest of the house because it was part of the gymnasium, a brick-built building set on its

46

own in the middle of the grounds. There was a swimming pool too, a cheerless rectangle of water that smelled of chemicals and feet.

'An indoor pool,' said Miss Thomas, who took Justice on a short tour of the facilities. 'You girls don't know you're born. In my day we had to break the ice on the outdoor pool.'

'Can we have games in the gym?' said one brave soul. 'It's still raining outside.'

'Nonsense,' said Miss Thomas who was, nevertheless, wrapped up pretty warmly in a fisherman's sweater over cricket flannels. 'You don't get wet if you run around.'

The girls, dressed in white aertex tops, brown sports skirts and long white socks, followed Miss Thomas out on to the field.

'You! New girl,' shouted Miss Thomas over the noise of the wind and the rain. 'Ever played lacrosse?'

'No,' said Justice. 'Lacrosse stick' had been on the list of equipment for Highbury House but, after buying it and lugging it all the way to school, Justice had managed to forget about the wretched thing.

'No, *Miss Thomas.*'

'No, Miss Thomas.'

'Well, we'll just practise catching and throwing at first. You'll soon get the hang of it.'

Except that Justice couldn't get the hang of it at all. The idea was to catch the ball in the net at the end of your lacrosse stick, hold it there (Miss Thomas called it 'cradling') and then pass it to another player. Justice had always thought breezily that she could use her superior tactical knowledge to master any kind of team game. But tactical knowhow is no good if you can't catch the ball – and Justice couldn't catch it, however hard she tried.

The other girls were patient at first but soon became tired of throwing the ball to someone who flailed wildly but seemed incapable of making contact.

'Come on, Justice,' said a girl called Susan. 'Try a bit harder.'

But she was trying. Tears of frustration mingled with the rain on Justice's face. Her knuckles hurt where the ball had hit her, and she had fallen over several times.

'Goodness,' Rose's voice wafted over from the neighbouring group. 'Justice is a bit of a rabbit, isn't she?'

Eventually, Miss Thomas separated the girls into two groups for a match. The blue team groaned when they were allotted Justice. She gritted her teeth and determined to show them. How hard could it be, after all?

Much harder than she could possibly have imagined was the answer. The game was so fast that Justice never even saw the ball, just flying figures hurtling along the pitch with their sticks aloft. Eventually she stopped trying to follow the action and stood still.

'Keep moving,' yelled Miss Thomas.

Justice jogged mindlessly along the edge of the pitch.

'Not that way!' shouted the teacher, her face alarmingly red.

Stella couldn't help her because, from what Justice could see, she was a good player, catching the ball at a run and passing it accurately. As for Rose, she was a ponytailed whirling dervish, scoring goal after goal. Twice Justice was sure that Rose deliberately aimed the hard ball at her. The second time she said, 'Ow! That hurt.'

'What?' Rose stopped, looking as innocent as an angel in a gym skirt.

'The ball hit my arm,' said Justice.

'Buck up, Justice,' said Miss Thomas, bounding over in her cricket jumper. 'We don't like whiners at Highbury House. Well played, Rose. You'd give the sixth formers a run for their money.'

Rose smirked and cantered off to score another goal.

'Played, Rose!' shouted the other girls adoringly. 'Well played, Rosie.'

At last the torture came to an end and Justice followed the other girls back into the changing room. She was soaking and muddy, her knuckles still hurt and there was a bruise on her leg where she had collided with someone's stick. *At least*, she thought, *I can have a bath now*. Surely this would be an exception to the once a week rule?

'Into the showers,' shouted Miss Thomas. 'Two minutes then out.'

The showers, cold and communal, were the worst experience yet. Afterwards Justice got dressed as quickly as she could. She never thought she'd be glad to put those long brown socks on. The cold water hadn't succeeded in washing off all the mud.

'Not so clever now, are you?' whispered a voice from the other side of the pegs. Coming after the disaster of the game, the words made Justice's eyes prickle. She couldn't see who had spoken because a towel hung in the way – but she could make a pretty good guess.

CHAPTER 6

After games they had tea – bread and butter and cocoa, which was the single best thing about Highbury House so far. Justice sat with Stella, who tried to be kind about the lacrosse debacle.

'It's a stupid game anyway,' said Stella. 'I much prefer hockey but Miss Thomas makes us play lacrosse because that's what they do at the famous schools like Roedean.'

'Did Miss Thomas go to Roedean?' asked Justice.

'No, she came here,' said Stella. 'So did Miss de Vere and Miss Morris. It's unhealthy really. Most of them have never been to another school.'

Justice remembered Miss Thomas's remarks about breaking the ice on the outdoor pool. Had she been at

Highbury House at the same time as Miss de Vere? The gym teacher, weather-beaten and high-coloured, could be any age, but Justice supposed that she might not be older than the headmistress. If Miss de Vere had taught Rose's mother she must be at least forty. Justice made a mental note to jot all this down later, then decided it was time to get down to business.

'Do you know anything about the maid that died?' she asked Stella, lowering her voice and leaning in slightly.

'No,' said Stella, looking slightly troubled. 'She just vanished. We all thought she'd been sacked. Then one morning we saw the undertaker's van drive up.'

'Do you know how she died?'

'No,' said Stella, then adding in a low voice, 'but Dorothy told Rose—'

'Why are you talking about me?' Rose called up from the end of the table where she was sitting with Alicia.

'Just saying how well you played today,' said Stella.

Rose eyed her suspiciously. 'Miss Thomas said I'll probably be captain of the team next year. You going to try out, Justice?'

'You're very good at lacrosse,' said Justice. A simple statement of fact can sometimes silence a hostile witness, that's what Dad always said. And it worked. Rose gave her a rather puzzled look and turned back to Alicia.

But now Stella was talking to Eva and Nora and Justice wasn't able to get the conversation back to Mary.

Justice had been planning a letter to her dad all day. She wanted to tell him exactly how bad Highbury House was. But, then again, she didn't want him to think that she couldn't cope. Ever since her mum had died this had been Justice's overriding concern. She mustn't be a burden on Dad. He had enough to worry about, with his work as a QC and everything, and without Mum to look after them both.

It had been all right before. Justice had had her mum for companionship and her dad to look up to. But now it was just her and Dad and that didn't seem enough for a family somehow. She thought enviously of Stella with her family of nine. *Nine*. With nine people there was safety in numbers – you could afford to upset one or two of them. But when it was just two of you, you had to be extra careful all the time. Maybe if she could solve the mystery of Mary's death, that would show her dad that she was a capable and competent person, and maybe, just maybe, he'd let her come home? She would tell Dad a little bit about the school and about Mary, but not enough to make him really worried. She'd try and be entertaining too, tell a story, just like Mum used to.

After tea they had to do 'prep', which turned out to be short for 'preparation' or homework. As Justice didn't have any to do, she started to write her letter.

Dear Dad,

I arrived safely yesterday. Highbury House looks like a cross between Dracula's castle and a lunatic asylum. I was driven from the station by a taxi driver who informed me that someone had recently died at the school. Great, I thought, at least I have a murder mystery to keep me going. Minutes later I met my first suspect, a sinister woman known as Matron

'Justice!' It was Stella whispering from the seat behind her. 'Justice, remember we have to leave our letters open so that Matron can read them.'

'What?' Justice turned round.

'Matron reads all our letters. You have to work out a code with your people. If I write 'quite' before a word my parents know I mean the opposite. "Rose is quite nice" and so on.'

Justice sighed, crumpled up her letter and started again.

Dear Dad,

I arrived safely yesterday. Highbury House is very impressive-looking — you can see it from miles away, rather like a famous castle in Transylvania.

I'm in a dormitory called Barnowls and I've met some very nice girls — Stella, Eva and Nora. And I've met Rose. The food brings a well-known Dickens novel to mind, although I didn't notice anyone asking for more. As do the bathrooms. Today I met Miss de Vere who seems very nice. She gave me Northanger Abbey to read. Please write and tell me how you know her? Also, VERY IMPORTANT, can you send a tuck box? This is FOOD. Pack things that don't go off like fruit cake, sardines and tinned peaches. If you're too busy, please ask Miss Lewis to do it.

Thank you.

With love from your daughter

Justice.

Much later, after Meal and ping-pong and a game of chess with Irene, Justice found herself back in the good old dormy. She was exhausted and the cast-iron bed with its grey blanket looked as enticing as a four-poster. After lights out, she switched on her torch and opened *Northanger Abbey*, which she had been carrying round in her satchel all day.

It opened easily because there was a note in it.

If you want to know what happened to Mary, meet me at the haunted tower, at midnight tomorrow.

Justice stared at the words, her heart thumping with excitement. 'At last,' she thought. 'I'm getting somewhere.'

If she could only prove there'd been a murder here, maybe Dad would let her leave Dracula's castle and come home.

CHAPTER 7

Justice began her preparations the next morning. In English, while the girls were reading aloud from *The Jungle Book*, she thought about the house and grounds. The tower was about five minutes' walk away, past the gymnasium and the old swimming pool. The difficulty would be getting out of the school without being seen. What would Leslie Light do? The trouble was that Leslie seemed to solve most of his cases sitting in an armchair in his Oxford college. Justice was just going to have to be more active about it.

When they were changing classrooms for the next lesson, Justice sneaked the note out of her book bag. The writing was clear and well-formed. A pupil, or someone pretending to be a pupil? It was written with a fountain pen in a rather distinctive blue-green ink. Justice resolved to look closely at her schoolmates' writing implements.

'Buck up, Justice,' said someone. 'You're blocking the corridor.' Justice stuffed the note back into her bag. 'Buck up' was one of the things they seemed to say a lot at Highbury House, along with 'look lively!' and 'shake a leg!' She always seemed to be in someone's way or late for something or other.

By the end of the day, Justice was getting very twitchy about her midnight appointment. As they walked to prep she saw Hutchins, the handyman, locking up, pulling the heavy bolts across the main door. But the little door inside it still seemed to be unlocked. Perhaps Hutchins used this door when he was carrying out his final night rounds? She hoped so. She might struggle to get out later, otherwise.

In prep Justice got to work. As soon as she arrived at Highbury House, she had begun work on a map of the place, adding details as she went. She looked at it now, adding the squeaky floorboards on the dormy corridor and the usual hours of Matron's rounds. She'd also drawn a rough plan of the grounds. She could see the tower from the dormy which meant that it was on the east side. She would have to skirt the gymnasium and approach through a small copse of depressed-looking trees.

'Stella,' she whispered. 'What happens at night?'

Stella looked up from her Latin translation. 'What do you mean?'

'Well, do you ever . . .' Justice sought for a suitable schoolgirl activity. 'Do you ever have midnight feasts or anything?'

Stella smiled. 'Sometimes. Matron does her rounds at night but she's normally finished by ten. She's got unnaturally good hearing though. You have to be quiet. Last term Eva got the hiccups and fell out of bed. We all got order marks and extra prep.'

'What about outside?' said Justice. 'Who patrols outside?'

'Outside?' said Stella. 'Why would you go outside?'

'When you've stopped gossiping, girls . . .' Justice looked up and saw that Helena Bliss had made a noiseless appearance by her desk. She gathered that it was normal practice for one of the prefects to 'take' prep, presumably so that the teachers could settle down by the roaring fire in their common room with a double brandy.

'Sorry, Helena,' said Stella.

'I don't want to give you an order mark,' said Helena.

Justice doubted that. She thought it would probably make Helena's week to give them an order mark. But an apology seemed to be the way to go. 'Sorry,' she said.

Helena gave her a hard look. 'I'll make allowances for you, Justice, because you're new and don't know how we behave at Highbury House.'

'Thanks.'

'Thank you,' corrected Helena.

'You're welcome,' muttered Justice as Helena drifted away in a cloud of what smelled like very expensive perfume.

It seemed as if the evening would never end but at last it was time for lights out. Justice didn't dare set her alarm. Instead she trusted in her ability to stay awake by reciting old murder trials.

Rex v Stanley. Man accused of murdering his friend over a poker game.

Rex v Donagh and West. Cousins accused of murdering elderly aunt for her money. One found guilty, the other acquitted.

Rex v Hamilton. Man who killed his wife and claimed that she had emigrated to Australia. Deception included dressing up in her clothes and travelling to Southampton docks.

Rex v Pewsey. A favourite. Housekeeper accused of murdering her employer. Evidence included remarks made by the deceased's parrot.

Gradually she heard the breathing in the room become regular. Eva started to snore, an annoyingly squeaky sound that had kept Justice awake into the early hours on the first night. Under the covers Justice shone her torch to check the time. Only ten o'clock.

Rex v Williams.

Rex v Hughes.

Rex v Bayliss and Bayliss.

Rex v Peruzzi.

Laura Peruzzi, a glamourous Italian actress, had been acquitted of murdering her unfaithful husband despite damning evidence against her. Justice's father had defended her. She remembered him describing the case to her and her mother. 'She just had to cry and say, in that wonderful voice, "I loved 'im." The jury was eating out of her hand.'

Squeak, squeak, from Eva. An owl hooted in the gloom outside. She heard someone passing the door, moving quietly on rubber-soled shoes. Matron on her rounds?

Rex v Goddard.

Rex v Gregory.

Rex v Cathcart.

At half eleven she was ready. She eased herself out of bed as quietly as she could and tiptoed over to her locker, where she had hidden her coat and outside shoes. Her school gabardine was in the closet on the ground floor, but Justice had had a presentiment that at some stage she would need to sneak out in the dead of night (as any good detective might), so she had secreted *this* coat in her dormy locker. With her outside shoes in one hand and her torch in the other, she crept out of the room. Rose moaned softly when Justice passed her bed but, thank goodness, she didn't wake up. *Probably having a nightmare that she had met someone with longer, blonder hair*, thought Justice.

The corridor was dark. Justice risked her torch and illuminated the bare boards and peeling paint. She passed the other dorms, taking care to avoid the loose floorboards. In Doves, someone was snoring so loudly that she could hear them from outside the door. She just hoped it wouldn't wake up the room's other occupants. She tiptoed down two flights of stone steps known as the maids' staircase, across the hall that led to the refectory, along the corridor where the servants' bells were, through the small room called Miss de Vere's sitting room, and into the main hall. There she stopped and silently put on her shoes.

The grandfather clock was ticking ponderously in the darkness. Justice thought about all the sleeping souls in the building. Was there also someone not sleeping, someone planning a rendezvous at the haunted tower? And was she, Justice, sufficiently prepared for the encounter? Well, it was too late for that now. She straightened her shoulders and with one last look to make sure nobody was around, she made her way over to the small door within the larger door and turned the handle.

She was in luck – it was open. Hutchins must still be on his rounds. The door gave a faint creak as it swung open and Justice winced, waiting to see if someone would come and she would be discovered. But the only sound was the ticking of the old clock. Steeling herself once more, Justice stepped out into the night.

Outside it was bitterly cold. Frost cracked under her feet and her breath froze in the air. *Still*, thought Justice as she set off, *it's not that much colder than the bathroom in the mornings.*

The moon shone so brightly that Justice didn't really need her torch, but she kept it clutched in her hand just in case. She glanced back at the school building. Highbury House, spooky enough in broad daylight, really was now doing its best to resemble Dracula's castle

– all dark, brooding turrets and small, sightless windows. Justice turned her back on it and trudged on towards the gymnasium. It was further than it had seemed when Miss Thomas had marched them there yesterday. Justice was soon shivering uncontrollably and she slipped a couple of times on the frosty grass. But before long she could make out the dark building, looming up out of the flat ground.

Like the main school, it seemed far bigger and more sinister than it had looked in daylight. Justice edged around it, keeping one hand on the brick walls, sheltered by the overhanging roof. At the back she stopped, just in time. In front of her was a huge crater, dark and apparently bottomless. Justice shone her torch into the space. It was a rectangular pit, large and obviously man-made. Some sort of animal trap? But then she remembered Miss Thomas's words: 'In my day we had to break the ice on the outdoor pool.'

Was this the old, abandoned swimming pool? Justice wondered, giving it a wide berth. If she fell in, she probably wouldn't be able to climb out again and the last thing she wanted was to be discovered at the bottom of the empty pool by the first games class of the morning. If she hadn't frozen to death in the night, that is.

The little copse of trees was in front of her now and, on the other side of it, the tower, a dark finger pointing to the sky. For a moment, forgetting that she was a fearless investigator, Justice had a sudden urge to turn and run, but she made herself go forward, one foot in front of another. The path was muddy here, beneath the trees, and Justice had to tread carefully, keeping the tower in sight.

Moonlight shone on the barred windows, making them glint and glimmer. Was this what Justice had seen from the dormitory the other night? She thought of Eva's ghost story, the girl dying in the tower. *You can still hear her crying at night sometimes.* Clouds drifted over the moon. *It must be nearly midnight by now*, she thought. She stood in the shadow of the trees at the edge of the wood, waiting. And then she heard it, in the distance, the first chime of midnight on the old grandfather clock.

Maybe her correspondent wouldn't turn up? Perhaps it was some new girls' tease and she'd arrive back at the dormy to find Rose and the rest of them crying with laughter, or else Matron waiting with her order-mark book. For a moment she almost hoped that was the case. But then, just as the chimes faded away, she heard footsteps.

Someone was walking towards the tower with a firm, decisive step. Her pulse quickening, Justice stepped back behind the nearest tree. She was suddenly very keen to see her visitor before they saw her.

The moon emerged once more from behind the clouds and the tower shone in an eerie light. Enough light, at any rate, for Justice to see Miss Thomas standing beside the wooden door with a grim and expectant look upon her face.

CHAPTER 8

Justice was immediately certain of one thing: she was not going to hang around for a cosy chat with her games mistress. She started to edge back through the trees. A twig cracked under her foot and Miss Thomas looked up. 'Who's there?' she called.

Justice turned and ran back to the school as fast as her legs could carry her, through the trees, round the pool, past the gymnasium, across the grass and up to the huge oak front door of Highbury House.

Justice breathed a sigh of relief as the handle turned. Thank goodness the little door was still open. She pushed it as quietly as she could and was just edging inside when she froze. She could hear footsteps. Someone was coming down the stairs. *Lucky the hall is full of large pieces of useless furniture*, she thought. Justice hid behind a trophy cabinet and tried to control her breathing. The footsteps came closer, a heavy masculine tread. *Hutchins*, she thought. He stopped in the hall and looked around, as if contemplating a last-minute check.

Don't look this way, prayed Justice. *Please don't look this way . . .*

Her prayer was answered. Hutchins made straight for the front door, a cold blast of air entering the hallway as he pulled the heavy door open and, after one last glance, pulled it shut behind him. Over the sound of her heartbeat Justice heard the key turn in the lock.

Justice let go of all the breath she'd been keeping in. The nearness of her escape made her feel faint. A few seconds later and she would have been discovered or – worse – locked out for the night. Quickly she took off her outdoor shoes and considered her retreat. It would be safer to go back via Miss de Vere's sitting room and the refectory corridor, but she suddenly had an overwhelming desire to be back in her bed. It would be quicker to go back by the main stairs. That route was riskier and more open, but who was going to see her at ten past midnight?

Shoes in hand, she bounded up the two flights of stairs and along the panelled landing that led to the dormitory corridor. She was just approaching the door when she stopped. Someone was coming towards her from the other side, walking very fast. *Not again*, she thought, panicking. *This place is like Piccadilly Circus.* She leapt towards a mahogany sideboard at the end of the landing and crouched down beside it just as the door swung open.

Justice hardly dared to breathe as feet clipped past her. Women's feet, wearing stout walking shoes. Justice didn't need her torch to identify the slim figure. It was Miss de Vere, wearing a black coat and hat. The headmistress ran down the stairs, her heavy shoes surprisingly light, and Justice heard the sound of a key in a lock. It must be the inner door. Yes, it made a soft, furtive click as it shut behind her.

Justice didn't wait to bump into anyone else. She hared along the corridor and, in seconds, was back in the dormitory, slipping gratefully into her own bed again.

Before she went to sleep, though, she took out her journal from its hiding place and, pulling the covers over her head, she wrote by the light of her torch –

THE MYSTERY OF HIGHBURY HOUSE SCHOOL AND
THE POSSIBLE MURDER OF MARY.

Assemble the facts and look for a pattern (Leslie Light).
MAIN SUSPECTS – SEEN OUT OF BED AT NIGHT :
1. Miss Thomas
2. Miss de Vere
3. Hutchins

'Justice! Wake up!'

'What?' Justice sat up. 'Where's Miss Thomas?'

Stella laughed. 'Things must be bad if you're dreaming about Miss Thomas. It's ten past seven. You slept through the bell.'

Ten past seven. Justice jumped up. She needed to get to the bathroom if she was to keep her place after Rose.

'Justice! Your *shoes*.'

Justice followed Stella's horrified gaze. Her outside shoes were by the bed, liberally caked in mud. She looked down – her pyjamas were also muddy at the bottom.

'I went out . . .' she began.

Stella's eyes grew wide. 'When? *Why?*'

Justice was aware of Eva and Nora hovering in the background and of the possibility of Rose appearing in her pink pyjamas to ask why they were all standing about like lemons.

'I can't explain now,' said Justice, then added in a whisper, 'Is there any time today when we can talk in private?'

'It's Wednesday,' said Stella, still eyeing her anxiously. 'We get the afternoon free. We can go for a walk if you like.'

'Great,' said Justice, kicking the muddy shoes under her bed.

Thank goodness she'd taken them off in the hall. There wouldn't be any muddy footprints to incriminate her at least, but she'd have to try and clean her pyjamas somehow. As soon as Rose returned, Justice dashed past her – eliciting a 'Hey, watch it!' as she grabbed her wash bag – and bolted for the Arctic bathroom before anyone else could notice.

As usual at Highbury House, free time was not quite what it sounded. There were no lessons but leisure options were strictly limited. They could go for a walk, but only in the grounds and only in twos or threes. They could do their prep or practise an instrument. They could read quietly in the library but no newspapers or magazines, if you please. And no detective stories. Improving novels only. The sixth form were allowed to go into the village. There was a rumour that Helena Bliss could drive and had once been seen at the wheel of her father's convertible. Justice dismissed this as fantasy; she didn't think that it would ever be warm enough on Romney Marsh to drive a convertible.

After lunch the girls were allowed up to the dormy to change into outdoor clothes. Stella kept watch while Justice sneaked into the bathroom and scraped the mud off her shoes with her nail file. She flushed the mud down the loo (the cistern gurgling for what seemed like hours) and rinsed the offending footwear under the tap. She also tried to wash the mud out of her pyjamas, which was less successful. The water turned brown but the material still looked dirty and the trousers were now wet from the knee down. There were no radiators in the upstairs rooms and so nowhere warm to dry them. Eventually, when no one was looking, Justice decided to hang them on the back of her locker door and hope for the best.

On the stairs she met Eva, who was at a loose end because her inseparable friend, Nora, had a dentist's appointment. There was a sticky moment when it looked as if Eva was going to accompany Justice and Stella on their walk. But, at the last minute, she decided that it was too cold and retreated to the library with a comic secreted inside her French vocabulary book. Stella and Justice signed out with Matron. Justice was terrified that Matron would look down and notice the mud on her shoes. But she didn't and a moment later . . . they were free. For a whole delicious hour.

They set off across the playing fields. It was a cold, bright afternoon but already, at just two o'clock, the shadows were lengthening.

'It'll be dark by three,' said Stella. 'I hate winter.'

Justice suddenly thought about Christmas, and how her mother always made a big thing of Advent. There used to be presents every day in December, just little things like sweets or a notebook or a handkerchief with a 'J' on it. This year she supposed that it would just be her and Dad.

'I hate winter too,' she said.

They walked in silence for a while. The field was dotted with other brown-uniformed girls walking in twos, but no one was in earshot. When they got to the end of the school grounds, they could see the marshes stretching in all directions, the seagulls swooping low over the mudflats. They stopped and leant on the fence. Justice screwed up her eyes, trying to see the sea. It was out there somewhere. Sometimes you could hear it whispering in the night. But now the grey waves merged with the grey fields and you couldn't see where one began and the other ended.

'So are you going to tell me why you were out wandering through the mud last night?' said Stella eventually.

It was surprisingly easy after that. Justice told Stella about the note and about her trip across the grounds at midnight.

'Goodness, Justice,' said Stella, looking sidelong at her. 'You're so brave. How did you have the nerve?'

'I just want to find out the truth about Mary,' said Justice. 'I wasn't particularly brave. You should have seen me running away after I saw Miss Thomas.'

'But do you really think it could be Miss Thomas who sent that note?' said Stella. 'I mean, she's a *teacher*.'

'I don't know,' said Justice. 'The person who wrote it said they knew something about Mary's death. But if that was Miss Thomas, why would she want to tell *me*?'

'But who else could it have been?' said Stella, her brow furrowed in thought. 'I mean, no one else was there last night.'

'Miss de Vere was,' said Justice. 'I saw her on my way back in. She was wearing outdoor clothes. She could have been on her way to the tower. And the note was in the book she gave me.'

'But she's the headmistress,' Stella almost wailed. She seemed incapable of believing that teachers could behave in surprising or underhand ways. Justice supposed that's what eight years of school did for you. She decided to try another tack. 'Let's look at it from the other way round,' she said. 'What do you know about Mary's death?'

'Not much,' said Stella, frowning again. 'I told you. We didn't even know she'd died till we saw the undertaker's van.'

'What about Mary herself? Did you ever talk to her?'

'Just once.' Stella kicked at a clump of grass. 'We're not meant to talk to the servants. I know it's horrible, but it's a rule. But one afternoon I saw Mary in the library. Maids aren't usually in the library so I asked her what she was doing. She said that Miss de Vere had asked her to sort through some old files.'

'When was that?'

'About a week before she died.'

'And she didn't seem ill at all?'

'No. I mean, I didn't talk to her for very long – Miss Thomas came in and told me off for talking to a servant – but she didn't look ill to me.'

'What was she supposed to have died of?'

'Pneumonia, I think. Eva heard Matron say so.'

Justice thought for a moment. 'Stella, what was the thing you were going to tell me, that Dorothy said to Rose?'

Stella looked confused.

'You know, when we last talked about Mary . . . you said that Dorothy told Rose something.'

'Oh, that!' said Stella. 'Oh, you know what Dorothy is like. She's a bit odd sometimes. She's got a bit of a crush on Rose, I think, and once she told Rose to be careful because . . .'

Stella's voice trailed off.

'Because what, Stella?' pressed Justice.

'Because there's a murderer in the school,' Stella finished in a whisper, her round eyes meeting Justice's. 'Oh, Justice, we all thought it was a joke. You don't think it's true, do you?'

Justice didn't want to scare Stella, but she didn't want to lie to her either. Unlike Rose and the other pupils of Highbury House, Justice had made a study of murder, and she was pretty sure this was no laughing matter.

Either way, she knew who she had to talk to next.

Matron was waiting for them when they got back, ticking names off her list.

'Please, Matron,' said Justice, trying to get the humble schoolgirl tone right, 'we got a bit muddy . . .'

'Whatever were you *doing*, Justice? Jumping in puddles?'

It was a clever plan to go out because now no one could prove that the mud on Justice's shoes was from last night rather than today, even though the playing fields weren't that muddy. Stella's shoes had hardly any mud on them at all. Justice couldn't help but feel pleased with herself. She was also hoping that Matron would send them off to the maids' quarters to clean up so that she could look for Dorothy. And sure enough, after a few choice remarks about carelessness, Matron told them to go to the pantry to clean their shoes.

The pantry was a cheerless room with stone sinks and huge cupboards, and worse – no Dorothy anywhere to be seen. Disappointed, Justice set to scraping the mud off her shoes, and smearing on red-brown Cherry Blossom polish.

'Whatever were you *doing*, Justice?' said Stella in what was such a spot-on impression that Justice looked up, half expecting to see Matron in the room. 'Shoe polish is expensive, you know. Girls these days have got no idea about household management.'

Justice tried to keep a straight face. 'Sorry, Matron,' she said, putting on a simpering voice. 'I'm just polishing my shoes so that they look as lovely as Helena Bliss's do. She cleans hers with angel dust, you know.'

Stella burst out laughing, and Justice couldn't help but join in. It was nice, she thought, to have a friend to do things with. It could make even cleaning shoes in a freezing-cold room seem quite fun.

'Girls! What are you doing?' A different voice, not Matron's thank goodness, but a French accent so strong that Justice often thought that it must be put on. Monsieur Pierre, the French master.

'Cleaning our shoes, Monsieur Pierre,' said Stella.

'It does not sound like it. It sounds like an 'orrible din.' Monsieur Pierre came further into the room and peered at them over the top of his little round glasses. He was the school's resident heartthrob which, as far as Justice was concerned, had everything to do with him being the only male teacher. She thought him very ordinary-looking, with his sandy blond hair, wispy moustache and glasses that made him look a little bit like a studious schoolboy. But she supposed that the only other man around was Hutchins, who looked like Frankenstein's monster's scarier brother.

Monsieur Pierre was now looking very intently at Justice's shoes. Despite her liberal application of polish, there was still quite a lot of mud around, on the shoes and on the floor.

'Where 'ave you been?' said the French master.

'We went to the end of the playing fields,' said Justice.

Monsieur Pierre narrowed his eyes. 'The only place where there is such mud is in the woods by the tower. Have you been out of . . . how do you say it? . . . out of bounders?'

'Out of bounds,' said Justice helpfully. 'No, we haven't been out of bounds this afternoon.' This wasn't a lie, she told herself, but maybe best not mention that she had been in the woods at midnight last night.

Monsieur Pierre eyed Justice for a moment, glasses glinting. 'Very well,' he said at last. 'Make haste. The bell for tea will be ringing shortly.'

So they made haste, but Justice couldn't help but wonder when Monsieur Pierre had last visited the muddy woods on the way to the tower.

At tea, Justice looked for Dorothy, hoping she might be serving, but there was only Cook pouring out cocoa and looking as if she wished it was liquid arsenic. Maybe it was Dorothy's afternoon off? Did she dare go into the scullery to check? Trying to avoid the teachers' gaze, Justice slipped out of her chair. She'd just managed to push the door open and was backing into the corridor when she bumped into Nora, arriving back from the dentist in Nye's taxi.

'There's a parcel for you,' she said. 'Matron's got it in her office.'

Justice raced upstairs. Could it be from her dad? She didn't want to hope.

When she got there, Matron was checking her laundry list.

'You aren't at tea, Justice.' Matron didn't look up.

'No, Matron.' Justice had learnt that, at boarding school, you were constantly being asked questions to which the answer was obvious. 'Aren't you tall?' 'Are you playing lacrosse?' 'Isn't your hair short?'

'Please, Matron,' said Justice, once again using her humble schoolgirl voice, 'Nora said you had a parcel for me.'

Matron continued to tick items off her list while Justice hopped from foot to foot in an agony of impatience.

'Don't fidget, Justice.'

Justice stood still and recited old murder trials in her head. Eventually Matron lifted a satisfyingly large parcel from the floor. 'It's from your father. Aren't you a lucky girl?'

'Yes, Matron.' She could see that the parcel had been opened.

'Are you settling in at school, Justice?'

'Yes, Matron.'

'You've made friends with Stella Goldman, I see.'

'Yes, Matron.'

'She's a nice girl, but don't put all your eggs in one basket.'

'No, Matron.' *What did that mean?*

'It's not always a good thing to have just one particular friend. They might let you down when you most need them.'

What was the answer to this? Why was Matron suddenly interested in her friendships? Justice said nothing and continued to look expectant. Thankfully, after looking at her intently for a few moments longer, Matron handed over the precious parcel. 'You'll have to take it to the kitchens,' she said, 'but you can keep some treats for your friends.'

'Thank you, Matron.'

At the Barnowls table, the parcel was treated with delight. Treat after treat was unwrapped from the Fortnum & Mason's paper: fruit cake, chocolate biscuits, Turkish Delight, sardines, tinned peaches, sausage rolls, fruit pastilles in a round tin with grenadier guards on the lid. Someone (Miss Lewis, probably) had even thought to include a tin opener.

'Justice,' breathed Eva, 'it's the best tuck box *ever*.'

'It's not bad,' conceded Rose.

Justice was glad that the tuck was so well received but she was disappointed that Dad hadn't enclosed a letter or anything personal. She supposed that he was too busy. Miss

Lewis must have chosen everything, wrapped and sent it. Well, she had done a good job.

'Is that tuck?' Another question of the completely unnecessary variety. This time it came from a red-headed girl who, judging by the badge on her blouse, was a prefect. 'You'd better put it away,' the prefect was saying. 'Only one item of tuck allowed at tea.'

'Have a sweet.' Justice proffered the grenadiers tin. From the intake of breath behind her she guessed that offering prefects sweets was another thing 'you just didn't do'. But the redhead just laughed and took a fruit pastille. Then she walked back to the sixth-form table.

'Did you see that?' said Eva. 'Pamela Powers took a sweet.'

'Yes, wasn't it simply *amazing*?' said Justice, rolling her eyes at Stella. 'Now, how do we smuggle this up to the dormy for a midnight feast?'

The Barnowls didn't even wait until midnight. As soon as Matron had soft-shoed her way past at ten, they sat on the floor with a torch in the middle of the circle and opened the tuck box. Justice saw Rose looking suspiciously at the mud on her pyjamas, but consuming fruit cake and peach slices seemed to have put the dormy captain into a mellow mood and for once she didn't say anything.

It was very cosy sitting huddled together with their blankets wrapped round them, but outside Justice could hear the wind howling. The windows rattled and somewhere deep in the house floorboards creaked and doors opened and shut.

'Let's tell ghost stories,' said Nora. Justice could see her glasses gleaming in the torchlight.

'Oh no, don't! It's too scary,' said Eva. She drank some ginger beer so fast that she started to hiccup.

'Don't be a rabbit, Eva,' said Rose.

'What about the haunted tower story?' said Justice, spotting her opportunity at last. Maybe this would give her a piece of the puzzle she needed to solve her mystery?

Eva moaned quietly but Nora was obviously keen to be the narrator. She pushed up her glasses and adjusted the torch so that it shone upwards on to her face, casting monstrous shadows on the ceiling.

'Many years ago,' said Nora, her voice low and urgent, 'this house was owned by a family called Highbury. That's why it's called Highbury House. Anyway, the Highburys had one child, a daughter called Grace. Grace was very beautiful, with very long blonde hair, and she was independent and wilful. Her parents wanted her to marry her wealthy cousin but Grace fell in love with the gardener, who was handsome and kind but very poor. When her parents found out, they were furious. Her father, Lord Highbury, ordered Grace to marry her cousin and, when she refused, he locked her up in the tower.

'She had no food or drink but she still refused to give up her true love. At night she wept bitterly and, towards the end, she cried out in agony but, of course, in the tower no one could her screaming. Eventually a servant broke in and found Grace dead, clasping a locket containing the likeness of the gardener. Her ghost haunts the tower. She's called the Blonde Ghost because her hair shines in the moonlight. Sometimes, at night, you can hear her sobbing . . .'

Everyone was staring wide-eyed at Nora, mouths open. Then they heard footsteps. Somebody was walking along the corridor outside; somebody with a slow, relentless tread. Eva gave a stifled scream.

'Matron . . .' Stella gasped, and switched off the torch.

The Barnowls sat in terrified silence. The footsteps stopped outside the door. Eva hiccupped and Rose put her hand over her mouth. Then, slowly, they heard the steady tread moving away towards the other dormies.

'Shh,' Rose warned. 'Don't move yet.'

It wasn't until they heard the door at the end of the corridor open and shut that they all breathed again.

'Phew! That was scarier than the ghost story,' said Stella, turning the torch on again.

'Quick, let's clean up in case she comes back,' said Rose, and they all sprang up, gathering the remainder of the food.

'Hide it in the laundry cupboard,' said Nora. 'There's enough for another feast.'

In less than five minutes the food was hidden away and the girls were in bed. For a moment the Barnowls all just lay there panting. Then Stella said, 'Thank you, Justice. That was a brilliant feast.'

'Yes, thanks, Justice,' murmured the others.

Justice lay there feeling . . . what did she feel? Breathless from the near miss with Matron, slightly scared (she had to admit) by the story and . . . well, happy. Happy that her dormy companions had enjoyed the feast, happy that they had shared a few moments of laughter – and of fear and tension too. *Maybe this is why people go to school?* she thought. *To share things*. It was a new idea, that there might be something good to say about Highbury House.

Justice felt for the grenadier guards tin under her pillow. She didn't know why she had put it there. Maybe it was just that the tin, with its little red-and-black soldiers, seemed like a message from Dad, something to comfort her when she put her hand on it in the night. She held the box tightly and then realised that there was something stuck underneath. She got out her torch. Yes, there was an envelope on the underside of the tin with 'Justice' written on it. She opened it and started to read.

I thought it safest to communicate in this rather clandestine way. But the secret of how I know Miss de Vere must wait until I see you on the half holiday. Hope boarding school isn't too boring. Perhaps you'll find some mystery to keep you entertained.

Veritas et fortitudo.

Dad

CHAPTER 9

Now Dad had said he was coming, Justice was longing for the half holiday. She tried not to count on it, because she knew how busy Dad was, but she couldn't stop herself. She was ticking off the days in her journal. Time seemed to behave strangely at boarding school. Sometimes it moved so slowly that she honestly wondered if the sands of time had run out altogether; when she was playing lacrosse on the freezing cold field, for example, or doing what Highbury House called 'science'. There were no laboratories at the school so the lessons consisted of reading textbooks written at the turn of the century, or laboriously drawing cross-sections of flowers under the gaze of Miss Loomis, the science mistress. At other times, when she was reading in the library or laughing at a joke with Stella, it would suddenly come upon her with a jolt: she had been at Highbury House for four weeks, a month.

It was slightly disconcerting to her to think that a newcomer to the school, seeing a girl in brown uniform crossing the quad or eating at the refectory, would think that she was just an ordinary schoolgirl and not an undercover agent bent on exposing a sinister murder plot. Sometimes Justice even forgot it herself. Mum always used to say that normal school life had a way of numbing your critical faculties, and Justice began to see that this was true. Before she knew it, Justice was caring about whether she beat Alicia in the maths test and openly speculating about who would have the lead part in the Christmas play.

And, yes, she did beat Alicia in the test. And, of course, the lead part in the play (the Angel Gabriel) went to Helena Bliss, with two prefects as supporting angels. Rose was an angel too, the only second former to be given this honour. 'Maybe it's because I look like Helena,' she kept saying. Justice thought that it was only a matter of time before Rose embroidered this on her school jumper.

The half holiday and the arrival of one's 'people' was all the girls could discuss. As far as Justice could make out, the occasion was a kind of grisly beauty contest with the entire school gathered in the refectory where visiting parents were forced to run the gauntlet of four hundred curious and critical eyes.

'It's terrible,' said Stella. 'Everyone looks to see if the mothers are wearing good furs and whether the fathers are going bald.'

'Are your parents coming?' asked Justice, thinking that at least her dad still had a full head of dark hair.

'No,' said Stella, her face falling. 'Just as well, I suppose . . .'

'Why?' said Justice. She could see that Stella wanted to say something else.

'Well, it's . . . hard,' said Stella, faltering. 'You know. With the other girls. I mean, my mum hasn't even got a fur, only an old trench coat.'

'Well, sucks to the other girls. My mother thought wearing fur was cruel,' said Justice.

Stella smiled at her. 'I'm glad you came to Highbury House, Justice,' she said.

Justice wasn't glad she came to Highbury House, and her only plan was to get away from the place as quickly as possible. And yet Stella's words gave her such a warm feeling inside that she couldn't help saying, on impulse, 'Why don't you come out with me and my dad?'

She had wanted Dad to herself, but Stella was really her only true friend here and she didn't want to condemn her to an afternoon of board games in the common room with Matron. She was rewarded by the look on Stella's face.

'Are you sure?' said Stella, brightening immediately. 'Don't you want some time alone with your father?'

'No, it's fine,' said Justice. 'He'll be pleased that I've made a friend.'

Until Highbury House, her only real friends had been her mother and Peter. She hadn't really felt the need for anyone else. But at boarding school, friends were essential, she realised. They were your protection, your status symbols, your light in the darkness. And, besides, it was nice, occasionally, to have someone to laugh with.

On the morning of the half holiday, the school was tense with excitement. Justice had noticed this before; it didn't take much for the girls to be overtaken by a kind of mass hysteria. Anything would do it – chocolate pudding for tea, a chance sighting of a man – but it was rather alarming while it lasted.

'I can't wait to see Mater and Pater,' said Nora, pushing back her lopsided glasses.

'It's only my mother coming for me,' said Eva, 'but it'll be jolly good to see her all the same.'

'It's rather a bore when my mother comes,' said Rose, spreading butter on her slab of bread. 'Because she was a pupil here everyone makes such a fuss of her. Matron, Miss Thomas and everyone. It's so embarrassing.'

Never, thought Justice, had anyone looked less embarrassed. 'Why not ask her not to come then?' she asked sweetly. 'Or tell her to put on a disguise?'

Rose shot her a distinctly unangelic look. 'Oh, I'm afraid my mother would stand out anywhere. She is a Beauty, you see.' She gave the word a capital letter as if it were an occupation. Or a disease.

'I can't imagine Matron making a fuss of anyone,' said Justice.

'Oh, Mother was best friends with Matron's daughter, Dilys,' said Rose. 'Matron adores her. And as for Miss Thomas, well . . . Mother was the star of the lacrosse team so you can just *imagine*.'

'What about Miss de Vere?' said Eva. 'Did she teach your mother?'

'Yes,' said Rose. 'She was the English mistress. But I don't think Mother really cared for her. She isn't all that keen on books, the mater.'

That figures, thought Justice. Rose wasn't stupid, exactly, but Justice had begun to notice that she did much better in tests when she was sitting next to the clever Alicia.

'And the pater's an important diplomat,' said Rose, rubbing it in. 'He's always in the London papers.'

'What about your father, Justice?' said Nora. 'Are you looking forward to seeing him?'

'Yes,' said Justice. In fact, she was looking forward to it so much that she'd woken up feeling quite sick.

'I bet he's old,' Rose whispered audibly to Eva.

But when Herbert Jones QC strode across the refectory, Justice could see that the girls were actually quite impressed. She supposed that her dad was presentable. He was tall and well dressed with all his own hair and teeth, but to her he just looked like a *dad*.

'Hallo, Justice.' At least he didn't attempt to do anything embarrassing like kiss her. 'Ready for the off?'

'Yes.' Justice stood up. 'Dad, this is Stella. She's going to come with us.'

'Wonderful,' said Dad, giving Stella a big smile and offering his hand. 'Glad to meet you, Stella.'

He seemed delighted that Justice had made a friend. Part of her was slightly offended (did Dad think she was so lacking in social skills?) but she was pleased that he was being so nice to Stella.

'Thank you for taking me.' Stella was blushing furiously but she managed to shake hands with tolerable composure.

'Let's go.' Justice wasn't about to introduce the rest of the Barnowls, even though Rose was tossing her hair for all she was worth.

On the way out, Justice saw a blonde woman who must have been Rose's mother being embraced by an effusive Miss Thomas. 'Dear Serena,' the games mistress was saying, 'how wonderful to see you.'

'Dear Tommy,' the woman was saying. *Tommy!* Justice stored that one up. Serena was accompanied by a grey-haired man, obviously Rose's important diplomat pater. Justice gave them both a very hard stare as she passed.

Miss de Vere was standing by the door being charming to passing parents. She held out her hand to Justice's dad.

'Mr Jones. How nice to see you.'

'Miss de Vere. Always a pleasure.'

Justice watched them closely. How come Dad and Miss de Vere were so friendly? And how did they know each other anyway?

'It's a pleasure to have Justice here,' said Miss de Vere. 'She's such a gifted girl.'

This was worth hearing at any rate. Her dad made some sort of modest noise and said, 'I've got your book in the car. Would you sign it when I bring Justice back?'

'I'd be delighted to.'

What was this? Had Miss de Vere written a book? Justice would have a lot of questions for her father when she could get him alone.

Most of the parents were taking their daughters to tea at The King's Arms, a depressed-looking hotel in Rye, but Justice's father had other plans. 'I thought we'd go on a tour,' he said, as they set off across the marshes. 'I've heard there's a place near here called Jury's Gap. I was intrigued by the name.'

Justice sat back, enjoying being in the warm car and seeing the grey fields flash past. It was lovely to be with Dad again too, his big hands on the wheel, his daredevil way of driving.

'Smashing car, Mr Jones,' said Stella from the back seat. 'What is it?'

'It's a Lagonda,' said Herbert. 'I call her Bessie.'

'We were going at thirty miles an hour then,' said Justice, keen to impress Stella with Bessie's prowess.

'Goodness,' said Stella.

Jury's Gap turned out to be a few cottages, hardly a village, clinging to the edge of the coast. They walked along the beach for a while, the sand stretching for miles, interspersed with streams and the occasional pool, bright blue in the afternoon sun.

'Shallow seas,' said Herbert, skimming a stone across one of the pools. 'There must be hundreds of shipwrecks out there.'

'Really?' said Justice, screwing up her eyes to look at the distant sea. She remembered her mum telling her a story about a haunted ship. *The Flying Dutchman* it was called. Perhaps Dad remembered it too because he suddenly took her arm. 'All right?'

'Yes,' said Justice. 'Of course I am.' Stella had tactfully walked away to examine some seashells.

'You miss your mum, I know,' he said quietly.

'Yes.' Sometimes Justice thought she would give anything to talk to someone about Mum. Now, for some reason, she just wanted Dad to stop. He gave her a quick squeeze and then let her go. Selecting another stone to skim, he said, in what seemed like a deliberately bright voice, 'Boarding school's not too bad, is it? Miss de Vere says you're doing very well academically.'

'How do you know?'

Dad threw the stone. It bounced once, twice, three times. He turned to Justice. 'She sent me a report. Just a standard thing.'

That didn't seem right. Questions raced through Justice's mind. 'Dad, how do you know Miss de Vere?'

Herbert laughed. 'Do you really want to know?'

'Yes,' said Justice patiently. 'Or I wouldn't have asked.'

'I represented her in a case.'

'Was it a divorce case?' asked Justice. She knew lots of people still thought divorce was shocking. That was probably why Miss de Vere had gone back to her maiden name. In case people like Rose's mother started gossiping.

'In a way,' said her father. She thought he was about to say more but, at that moment, Stella came back with a hatful of seashells.

'Let's go and have some lunch, shall we?' said Herbert.

They ate at a funny little pub that was like the inside of a ship. Justice and Stella had fish and chips. No, they assured Justice's father, they wouldn't be spoiling their supper because supper was called Meal and Meal was probably just dead baby anyway. 'Dead baby?' said Herbert. 'Good God.' He drank a thoughtful sip of beer.

Stella was now telling Justice's father about her family. 'There are seven of us children,' she was saying. 'Dad's a solicitor so he doesn't earn much.' She blushed again. 'I mean, a solicitor's not like a QC.'

'What's his name?' said Herbert.

'Joshua Goldman.'

'Oh, I know him. He's a good man.'

Stella's face lit up at that. She seemed to like Dad, thought Justice. She told him stories about her mother making all their clothes and once sewing the wrong name on her gym kit. 'My sisters are Sarah and Sheila so she gets confused.' Herbert laughed and Justice joined in. She was pleased that Dad seemed to like Stella but she couldn't help feeling slightly put out all the same. When was she going to get Dad on his own? But then, if they were on their own, would he try to talk about Mum again? She wanted to tell Dad about Mary's death, but would it be better if she just solved the mystery on her own and presented him with the finished results, the way Leslie Light would? She dithered, eating her chips slowly and listening to Stella talking about Christmas with the Goldman family.

And then, before she'd quite decided what to do, Herbert was looking at his watch and saying that he had to get them back. 'No later than six, that's what it said in the letter. We'd better get motoring.'

It was already dark outside when they left the pub and began the journey back across the marshes. It was like being in space, thought Justice, or under the sea. Blackness, nothingness, all around them, just the occasional glimmer of lights on the horizon. Dad hummed under his breath and Stella was silent in the back. Justice never wanted the drive to end.

But there was Highbury House looming up out of the landscape, seemingly blacker than the night itself. Stella thanked Justice's father for the afternoon and then hurried into the school, leaving them on their own.

'Goodbye then, Justice.'

'Bye, Dad.'

He kissed her on the cheek. 'Don't forget to write to me. Your letters seem a bit stilted sometimes.'

'That's because Matron reads them,' says Justice. 'We need a code.'

She could see that this appealed to Dad. His face, which had looked serious at the mention of Matron reading the letters, brightened. 'If you need my help,' he said, 'just write "Peter's playing the Bach" and I'll come immediately. I promise.'

'All right,' said Justice.

Dad looked like he was about to say more when a voice called, 'Mr Jones?'

It was Miss de Vere, striding towards them. 'Did you want me to sign a book?'

'I certainly do.' Dad dived into the car and came out with a leather-bound book. Miss de Vere took a pen out of her bag and signed on the title page.

'I do hope you enjoy it.'

'I'm sure I will. Look, Justice.'

He showed her the inscription. Justice looked. And looked again. It wasn't the signature that caught her attention, although it revealed the fascinating fact that Miss de Vere was called Dolores.

No, it was the *ink*. A distinctive blue-green ink. Exactly the same ink used in the note asking her to meet in the tower at midnight.

CHAPTER 10

Justice couldn't wait to tell Stella. As soon as Matron had ticked her name off on one of her endless lists, Justice raced to the common room where Stella was sitting reading a book. Rose, wearing what was obviously a new fur hat, was regaling her fans with an account of her day with The Beauty and The Diplomat.

'Stella . . .' said Justice.

Stella looked round.

'Can I talk to you for a minute?' said Justice, adding in a whisper, '*in private.*'

Stella looked confused but followed her back out on to the landing. Justice led the way to a funny little room that she'd found when trying to complete her Highbury House map. It was scarcely more than a cupboard and was, apparently, directly underneath the North Turret. They went in there now and sat on boxes marked, 'Electrical. Do not Touch.'

'What is it?' said Stella, sounding rather grumpy. *Never mind*, thought Justice, *she'll cheer up when she hears the news.*

'Miss de Vere wrote the letter!'

'What letter?'

'The letter telling me to meet her at the tower! Well, at least it was written with the same pen. I couldn't really tell about the handwriting because signatures are different, but it was definitely the same ink – the colour is quite distinctive. I need to get into Miss de Vere's office somehow and see if I can find any more clues. Maybe one of the teachers killed Mary and she knows . . .'

'Justice!' Stella sounded almost angry now. 'You can't really believe that Miss de Vere wrote that letter.'

'Why not? It was her pen.'

'Teachers don't do things like that.' Justice remembered Stella saying something similar about Miss Thomas. But teachers were just people, weren't they?

'I think she did,' said Justice. 'And whether that means

she knows who the murderer is, or is the murderer herself, I'm going to prove it. My father says—'

'Your father wouldn't want you to break school rules.'

'How would you know?' snapped Justice. 'You only met him today.'

Stella's face went white. She looked as if she was about to speak but then turned and left the room without another word.

Justice didn't get a chance to speak to Stella until they were in the dormy, getting ready for bed. She wished she had more experience of friends. What did you do when you'd upset a friend but didn't know why? Did you apologise? Or say nothing and hope the upsetness would just go away? In the end, when they were drawing the curtains at the far end of the room, Justice said, 'I'm sorry if I upset you earlier.'

To her surprise Stella said, 'I'm sorry too. It was just . . . I'd had such a nice day with your dad, it made me miss my family. That's why I got cross.'

'That's all right,' said Justice. 'I understand.' Justice realised she did understand. Somehow the day with Dad had made her miss Mum all over again.

'About Miss de Vere—' Justice began.

'What are you whispering about?' said Rose from the other end of the room. 'Lights out in five minutes.'

'Let's talk about it tomorrow,' whispered Stella

'Let's,' said Justice. 'All right, Rose. I'm getting into bed now.'

It was a relief to get under the covers. The dormy was colder than ever.

'Hutchins says it's going to snow soon,' said Eva from across the room.

'I like snow,' said Justice, trying to warm her freezing feet by rubbing them together.

'You don't know what it's like here,' said Nora in her spectral ghost-story voice. 'We're completely cut off if it snows. A few years ago, it snowed so hard that none of the tradespeople could get through and we nearly ran out of food. We ate bread and dripping for weeks.'

'The water freezes too,' said Eva, 'and we can't wash in the mornings. It's so cold that you can see your breath, even in bed.'

'We did build a smashing snowman though,' said Nora. 'We put a hat on it and called it Monsieur Pierre.'

'Lights out,' came Rose's voice, as everyone else giggled. And darkness descended on the Barnowls.

*　　*　　*

The weather got colder and colder. There was ice on the inside of the bathroom windows and most of the girls had coughs or colds. Worse still, the tuck had run out and food in the dining room seemed sparser than ever. Eva said it was because Cook was stocking up in case they got snowed in.

The thought of snow started to make Justice feel uneasy. If it snowed a lot, they would be trapped in Highbury House, possibly in the company of a murderer. She had felt odd, anyway, since the day at Jury's Gap. Seeing Dad had made her miss him more than ever and she was still a bit upset about the row with Stella. Friends were essential, she knew that now, and it seemed that if you weren't careful you could lose them as quickly as you found them.

Worst of all, after the exciting revelation about the pen, Justice wasn't making any headway at all in her investigations. She had been up to Miss de Vere's room several times, but she was always in there, or else the door was locked. Justice was beginning to wonder if she should just ask the headmistress outright, when fate took a turn.

It was a week after the half-term holiday. Justice was walking slowly to English. She didn't think it was worth hurrying. All they seemed to do these days was practise the

Christmas play. Justice was the narrator. She already knew her part by heart and was thoroughly bored. 'And it came to pass in those days that a decree went out from Caesar Augustus . . .'

'At least you don't have to simper and say, "I am the handmaid of the Lord" when Helena Bliss waves a scroll at you,' said Stella, who was playing Mary. Most of the big speeches in the play went to Gabriel and her hench-angels, and Helena, of course, would be singing too, accompanied by Irene on her screechy violin.

Besides, this morning most of the other girls, Stella included, had been waylaid by Miss Thomas to discuss a forthcoming lacrosse match. Justice was one of only two girls in the form not in the team. Even Joan, who had one leg shorter than the other, was the reserve.

Justice walked along the corridor, thinking about her latest letter from Peter. He wrote to her quite often and she felt badly that she had been so wrapped up in her mystery that she hadn't replied for an age. He mostly wrote about music, often including scraps of score she couldn't read, but in his last letter he'd talked about the Christmas holidays. 'Mother says you and your dad can come to us,' he wrote. 'Should be fun, although I'll have to practise the Bach in the afternoon.' Was this what she and her dad had become?

thought Justice. Refugees invited to other families out of pity? It made her wish that she could cook Christmas dinner herself.

She was just reluctantly starting up the twisting steps that led to the English classroom when she heard a voice calling her name.

'Justice!'

An authoritative, teacher-ish voice. Justice turned. It was Miss de Vere herself, holding a stack of books.

'Yes, Miss de Vere?'

The headmistress smiled at her. 'Miss Crane isn't very well today so I'll be taking your English class. Could you give me a hand with these books?'

Justice brightened. Here was a chance to talk to Miss de Vere. She might be able to get the subject round to the tower and secret notes. Or, if Miss de Vere was the one who sent the note, maybe the headmistress was looking for an excuse to speak to Justice in private?

Justice took the books proffered by Miss de Vere. They were new hardbacks, blue with a black silhouette of a horse and a rider. They looked unlike anything ever seen in Highbury House, where the Shakespeare volumes looked as if they might have come from Will's own personal collection.

'I thought we'd read something new today,' said Miss de Vere as they climbed the stairs. 'Have you ever heard of *National Velvet* by Enid Bagnold?'

'No,' said Justice.

'No, Miss de Vere.'

'No, Miss de Vere.'

'It's a thrilling book,' said Miss de Vere. 'Only published last year. It's about a girl who disguises herself as a boy to ride in the Grand National. I think you'll enjoy it.'

Justice wondered if the word 'thrilling' had ever been used before by a Highbury House teacher. And as for the notion of 'enjoying' a book, she was pretty sure that the concept would be alien to Miss Crane, whose only ambition seemed to be to force her pupils to memorise as many lines of classical literature as possible. And she liked the idea of a girl riding in a famous horse race. Why should boys have all the adventures? Living in London, Justice had only seen horses at a distance, being ridden by policemen or cantering down Rotten Row in Hyde Park. She couldn't imagine what it might be like to ride one of those beautiful, terrifying creatures.

They reached the classroom and Miss de Vere handed Justice the rest of the books so she could open the door. She looked round at the empty desks and chairs.

'Goodness! Where is everyone?'

'At a lacrosse meeting,' said Justice, putting the books on the teacher's table.

'And you don't play lacrosse?'

'I'm forced to play it,' said Justice. 'I'm just not very good at it.'

Miss de Vere laughed. She sat at the table on the dais and smoothed out her gown.

'Are you enjoying boarding school, Justice?'

'Sometimes,' said Justice truthfully.

'You seem to have made friends,' said Miss de Vere. 'I'm very happy to see that you've teamed up with Stella.'

What was this obsession with teams, thought Justice. And why was Miss de Vere asking her all these questions? Did she realise that Justice suspected her of sending that note? Did she want her to know? Or was it possible that she hadn't sent the note? Maybe someone else had the same colour ink . . .

Justice decided to embark on some subtle questioning.

'Miss de Vere?' she said. 'What was the book you wrote? The one you signed for my Dad?'

'It was a book about Jane Austen,' said Miss de Vere. 'Did you enjoy *Northanger Abbey*?'

'Sort of,' said Justice. 'Catherine Moreland seemed a bit slow on the uptake sometimes.'

'But she has a wonderful imagination,' said Miss de Vere. 'And imagination can be a great gift. Just don't let it run away with you, as Catherine did.'

There was clearly some kind of message here, but Justice couldn't quite decipher it. Did the headmistress know about her investigations into Mary's death? If she sent that note, she definitely did. Was she trying to imply that Justice had made the whole thing up?

'Miss de Vere,' she said, 'how come you know my father?'

That change again. The headmistress's face was still poised and pleasant but something was different, as if an internal light had been turned off.

'Don't ask impertinent questions, Justice. You can give out the books. One on each desk.'

'It must be wonderful to write a book,' Justice tried again. 'Could I have your signature or a motto to put in my autograph book?' Justice didn't have an autograph book but lots of the girls did. They were full of sayings like, 'Be good, sweet maid, and let who will be clever.' If she had a longer sample of Miss de Vere's writing, she could compare it to the note. Handwriting could be an important clue; she knew that from all the murder trials she'd read.

'No,' said Miss de Vere. 'Hurry up with the books.' And, at that moment, the lacrosse team galumphed into the room.

At the end of the lesson, Justice volunteered to clean the blackboard, thinking that she might get a chance to see Miss de Vere's writing on the register, but the headmistress just swept out of the room with her gown billowing after her. Justice was left wiping away the words 'simile', 'metaphor' and 'atmosphere'. It was some moments before she realised that there was someone else in the room.

'You never came,' said a voice flatly.

Justice spun round. Dorothy was standing there, duster in hand.

'What?' she said.

'You didn't come. That night. To the tower.'

Justice stared. 'That was you?'

'Yes,' said Dorothy.

'I've been wanting to talk to you anyway!' said Justice, getting excited now. 'About what you said to Rose.'

'What did I say to Rose?' Dorothy looked scared now, as if Justice was going to tell her off for being impertinent.

'You said that there was a murderer in the school.'

Dorothy tilted her chin and, for the first time, looked Justice in the eye. 'I think there is. And, as you're the only one who's ever been interested in Mary, I wanted to tell you.'

'Tell me what?'

Dorothy looked nervously around the classroom but there was no one else there. Justice could hear someone practising scales in the music rooms above.

'I think I know who killed her,' said Dorothy.

CHAPTER 11

'What?' Justice stared while, above them, the scales continued: up and down, up and down. 'I mean, who?'

'I think it was Miss Thomas.'

'Miss Thomas! Why?' whispered Justice. 'Why would you think that?'

'I can't talk now,' said Dorothy. 'Will you meet me tonight?'

'All right,' said Justice. 'But not at the tower again. It was a nightmare getting there and, besides, everyone says it's going to snow tonight.'

'Can you meet me in my room? It's in the attic. No one goes that way at night. I used to share it with Mary but now I'm on my own.'

'All right.'

'At midnight?'

'Why do you keep suggesting midnight?' said Justice. 'It's so hard to stay awake. What about eleven o'clock?'

'It's always midnight in the books,' said Dorothy.

So Dorothy was another fan of gothic horror! 'All right,' said Justice. 'Where's your room?'

'At the top of the servants' staircase. On the way to the North Turret. You can't miss it. I've got to go.' And, with a final terrified glance over her shoulder, Dorothy whisked away.

The snow started in earnest during prep. The girls kept jumping up to look out of the window despite the protests of Pamela Powers, who was meant to be in charge.

'Sit down,' she kept saying. 'Anyone would think that you'd never seen snow before.'

Justice didn't think she had. Snow in London tended to be a well-behaved affair, a light dusting on the rooftops of St John's Wood, barely enough to scrape together a snowball or build a small snowman. But, here, you could already see whiteness as far as you looked, the marshes glowing with a faint blue light in the darkness. People talked about being cut off, about food running out, about Hutchins going to the village on a sled. The snow talk made Justice feel slightly

114

scared. If she was going to be marooned, this wasn't exactly the company she would have chosen. She shuddered at the thought of being snowed in all winter with Rose and Helena Bliss. Justice had read about an Arctic expedition where the explorers had been so hungry they had started eating each other. She could just imagine Rose and company descending on some poor first year, knives and forks at the ready. Well, she wasn't about to be anyone's main course, thank you very much.

And that wasn't even to mention Miss Thomas – a murderer, if what Dorothy said was to be believed. Justice knew it was wrong, and of course what happened to Mary, if it was true, was awful. But she couldn't help but be a little bit excited. A real murder mystery, her first proper witness, and at last – someone to talk about it all with. Midnight couldn't come soon enough.

By the time they went to bed, the snow had almost reached the ground-floor windows. They all crowded round the far window, which had the best view over the marshes.

'We'll be snowed in for days,' said Eva.

'It's rather beautiful,' said Stella. And, looked at objectively, the scene *was* beautiful: the smooth white expanse glittering in the moonlight, the tower standing dark and sinister, snowflakes swirling round its battlements. But Justice didn't feel very objective. She couldn't shake a bad feeling about the snow. And it wasn't just because Rose kept going on about wearing her fur hat and cape tomorrow.

At least the Barnowls fell asleep fairly quickly, worn out by all the excitement. As soon as Justice was absolutely sure no one was awake, she slipped out of bed, opened the door quietly and stepped into the corridor.

There was not a sound to be heard. It was as if the snow outside had cast a cloak of silence on the school. Justice tried to make her feet soundless too, avoiding the creaking floorboards, moving like one of Nora's ghosts. At least this time she didn't have to go outside. All she had to do was get to the landing and take the maids' staircase upwards. But as she reached the end of the corridor, she stopped. Footsteps, rubber-soled and purposeful.

Matron.

Justice flattened herself against the wall. If Matron saw her, she'd have to pretend to be sleepwalking. But then the footsteps stopped and she heard Matron say, 'What are you doing here?'

A man's voice answered. 'I wanted to see ze snow from ze North Turret.' Justice would recognise that overdone French accent anywhere.

'You can't go to the turret,' said Matron. 'It's locked.'

'My apologies. *Bonne nuit.*' *Bonne nuit!* Who was he trying to kid? Justice thought Matron wasn't impressed either. She heard her snort before (thank you, God!) going back into her room, which was next door to the sickbay. Justice waited until Monsieur Pierre's footsteps had died away before carrying on down the landing. But just as she was at the door that led to the attic staircase at the foot of the North Turret, she heard someone descending the stone stairs very fast. What now?

Justice dived behind a curtain. It wasn't ideal but it would have to do. The door opened and, through the threadbare velvet, she saw Miss de Vere fully dressed and looking very serious. The headmistress paused, so close that Justice could smell her perfume, but after a moment she set off again and Justice could hear her heeled boots clicking their way downstairs.

Where was the headmistress going? If Dorothy had written the note, it meant that Miss de Vere hadn't been heading out to meet Justice the other time, the time Miss Thomas had been waiting by the tower. So, why *was* she always prowling around at night? And why was she visiting the North Turret which was meant to be locked? Justice thought of Monsieur Pierre, with his pale moustache and exaggerated accent. Was Miss de Vere going to meet him? Were they – revolting thought – *in love*?

With all these teachers around, Justice was tempted just to go back to her dormy, but Dorothy was waiting for her, so after a few more minutes, once she was sure the house was completely silent, Justice tiptoed out from her hiding place and started climbing the attic stairs.

'I thought you weren't coming.'

'It was a bit busy out there,' said Justice. 'I came as soon as I could.'

A month ago, she would have been shocked at Dorothy's room, reflected Justice, but now she couldn't help thinking that it was nicer than the dormy. It was much bigger, for one thing, and Dorothy had it all to herself. Mary's bed was an ominously shrouded shape in the corner. Dorothy's bed was like Justice's, narrow with an iron frame, but there was a patchwork quilt on it and a large teddy bear (two items that would definitely be confiscated by Matron). Seeing the bear made Justice wonder how old Dorothy was.

'Fifteen,' said Dorothy when Justice asked. 'I've been working here for a year.'

That made Dorothy three years older than Justice. She tried to imagine what Dorothy's life was like. Awful as it was to come to Highbury House as a pupil, what must it be like to be here as a servant, forced to work from dawn to dusk, being despised by girls like Rose who were so much younger than her? She heard Rose's voice, those confident cut-glass vowels. 'Look out, it's Dotty Dorothy.' Judging by the books on Dorothy's bedside table, she certainly read more than Rose, whose main reading was back copies of *Tatler* magazine.

'Do you like it here?' asked Justice.

Dorothy shrugged. 'It's all right. It can be a bit spooky at night, especially now I'm sleeping on my own. Last night I thought I heard voices coming from the North Turret, but I must have been imagining it as that room's always kept locked.'

Justice suddenly heard Monsieur Pierre's voice . . . *I wanted to see ze North Turret* . . . Could he be up to something? Matron had said it was locked too. Despite herself, Justice shivered.

'The pay's not bad,' Dorothy continued, 'and you get food and lodging too. It's hard work though.'

'What do you do?'

'I have to make the teachers' beds and lay the fires, help Cook in the kitchen, wash up after meals, sweep, polish, clean shoes, feed the pigs. I do have Sunday afternoons off though.'

'Goodness.' Justice felt quite exhausted at just the thought of it all. 'Why do you . . .' She stopped, not knowing quite how to continue.

'Why do I work here? I'm the oldest of five so I had to leave home and earn some money. I do miss my mum though.'

'I miss mine too,' said Justice. She wasn't quite sure why she'd said it; she had spent all of her time at Highbury House avoiding talking about her mother and now here she was confiding in someone she'd only known for a few minutes.

'She's dead, isn't she?' said Dorothy. 'I heard some of the teachers talking. I'm ever so sorry.'

'That's all right,' said Justice, as she always did.

'It's not though, is it?' said Dorothy, her hazel eyes sympathetic.

'No, it's not,' said Justice.

Funnily enough, this seemed to make the atmosphere easier and Justice was able to curl up on Dorothy's bed and say, 'So what's this about Miss Thomas?'

Dorothy sat next to her and pulled the patchwork quilt over them. It was extremely cold in the attic.

'Mary was ill,' she said. 'She had a cold or something. She was coughing so much that Mrs Hopkirk . . . the housekeeper,' she added, seeing Justice's blank look, 'sent her to bed. I saw her that night and I made her hot lemon and honey. She was all right. Ill, but not too ill, if you know what I mean. We played cards and she said she felt hungry. My mum always says that's a sign you're on the mend. Well, next day Mary stayed in bed but mostly because Mrs Hopkirk said she could. I came up to see her at lunchtime and I saw Miss Thomas coming out of our room. I was really surprised to see her there. Miss Thomas said that she'd come to see how Mary was.'

'I suppose that could have been true,' said Justice.

'Except that, afterwards, Mary was really ill. She had a temperature and kept saying this odd thing – that the fog was coming down and she couldn't see. I was scared and I called Matron. She took Mary to sickbay and she died that night. Pneumonia, they said it was. But I found a glass next to her bed and it had all this powdery stuff in it. I think Miss Thomas poisoned her.' Dorothy sat back, looking at Justice to see her reaction. 'When Mary had her fever she said something about Tom. At first I thought he must be her brother but now I think it was Miss Thomas.'

'Miss Thomas was at the tower that night,' said Justice. 'That's why I went away without meeting you.'

'I was late,' said Dorothy. 'It was deserted when I got there.'

'But if Miss Thomas was there, she must have known about the note. Where did you write it? Could Miss Thomas have seen you?'

'When I was cleaning Miss de Vere's office. I used her pen.'

I knew it, thought Justice.

'But could Miss Thomas have seen you write it?'

'I don't think so.'

'Maybe she just followed us.'

'But do you really think she's a murderer?'

'The evidence certainly points that way,' said Justice carefully, 'but we'd need much more to prove it. I don't suppose you kept the glass with the powder?'

'No, it all happened so fast, I just didn't think.'

'Pity. Now, we must look at this logically. A jury probably wouldn't convict on purely circumstantial evidence. We need something more solid. I'm going to ask my dad.'

'No!' Dorothy jumped up. 'You can't tell your father. I'd get into terrible trouble. I'd lose my job.'

'Don't worry,' said Justice. 'My dad knows about murder. He's a barrister. He'll be able to help us find some evidence.'

'But you can't write to him. Matron reads all the letters. I've seen her.'

'I'll use a code,' said Justice. 'We worked it out on the half holiday. If I write, "Peter's playing the Bach", it means I need his help immediately. He'll come down. You'll see.'

'But it's snowing,' said Dorothy. 'The post won't get through.'

'We'll just have to hope that it doesn't snow any more,' said Justice. 'I'd better be going. It's nearly one o'clock.'

'All right,' said Dorothy rather reluctantly. Justice got off the bed but Dorothy grasped her arm. 'Listen!'

'What?'

Then Justice heard it too. Footsteps outside, soft padding footsteps. The passage led only to the maids' bedroom and the turret. Someone must be coming to see Dorothy.

Dorothy clutched Justice's arm. 'It's Miss Thomas!'

'It can't be. Shh.' Justice crept to the door and looked through the keyhole. There, framed in moonlight from one of the narrow windows, she saw an angel. A girl with long blonde hair, barefoot, dressed in white. At first Justice thought it must be Rose, that Rose had followed her from the dormy, but then, with a shock that made her heart beat a bit faster, she saw that it was Helena Bliss. Helena in her nightdress, standing motionless as if she was listening. Justice could smell her perfume wafting under the doorway.

Why had Helena Bliss put on scent to go wandering the corridors at night?

Justice stayed frozen at the keyhole, motioning at Dorothy to keep quiet. For what seemed like hours, Helena stood there, looking around her. At first it seemed as if she was glowing with some unearthly light but then Justice saw that she was simply carrying a torch in one hand. Slowly Helena shone the torch up and down the corridor. Justice saw the light seeping under Dorothy's door and held her breath. But at last Helena seemed satisfied and set off, not towards the stairs but towards the North Turret.

Finally they heard a door open at the end of the corridor. Justice let out her breath with a long sigh. Then she turned to Dorothy. 'It was Helena Bliss.'

'Miss Bliss? The head girl? What was she doing here?'

'I don't know,' said Justice. 'But I don't like it.'

'She's ever so beautiful, isn't she?' said Dorothy. 'Like an angel.'

But angels didn't wander about at night drenched in perfume, thought Justice. She didn't think that there was any point in saying this to Dorothy.

Back in her dorm bed, Justice got out her journal.

The mystery deepens. Dorothy thinks that Miss T murdered Mary. From what I've seen of Miss T it seems possible but — NO EVIDENCE.

Then again — why was Miss T at the Tower that night?

Why was Helena B in the North Turret corridor tonight?

Also Miss de V's behaviour continues to be suspicious. She didn't write the note asking to meet me in the Tower (D wrote it with her pen) so why was she there at all? I'm not sure what I think about Miss de V. She can be nice one moment (e.g. talking about books) then cold and scary the next. Also I never found out exactly how Dad knows her.

It's snowing. This makes me scared though I'm not sure why. Maybe just because there's a chance that we could be completely cut off here at H House. Not to mention the fact that it makes the dormy colder than ever.

On the plus side, I think I've made a new friend.

She thought for a moment and added a few names to her list:

MAIN SUSPECTS — SEEN OUT OF BED AT NIGHT:

1. Miss Thomas (number 1 suspect)
2. Miss de Vere
3. Hutchins
4. Monsieur Pierre
5. Matron
6. Helena Bliss

Justice sighed. That was a long list. Tomorrow she would have to start narrowing it down.

CHAPTER 12

It was obvious at breakfast that something was wrong. Most of the girls were too busy squealing about the snow but Justice noticed the teachers were all standing at one end of the refectory, talking intently. Matron was there too, and Hutchins.

'*Benedictus benedicat,*' said Helena Bliss and the clamour of eating began. Justice thought the head girl looked rather pale but she seemed her usual composed self at the head of the prefects' table. What *had* she been doing in the attic last night?

There was another clamour as chairs went back and everyone stood up while Miss de Vere came into the room.

'Sit down, girls,' said the headmistress with a smile. Then she went over to join the group of teachers.

'What do you think they're talking about?' Justice asked Stella. She hadn't yet had a chance to tell Stella about last night's adventures.

'Maybe about the snow,' said Stella. 'To see if we can do games this afternoon.'

It was Saturday, which meant compulsory games all afternoon. Justice prayed that the snow was five feet deep on the playing fields.

'Of course we'll do games,' said Rose. 'We're not going to be put off by a bit of snow.'

'If they're talking about games,' said Justice, 'how come Miss Thomas isn't there?'

They all looked towards the teachers. Miss Crane, Miss Bathurst, Miss Morris and Monsieur Pierre were all in a huddle, muttering to each other in low voices. Hutchins stood on the margins of the group, his arms hanging at his sides, clearly feeling uncomfortable. Matron and Miss de Vere seemed to be in charge and were now obviously conferring.

Miss de Vere clapped her girls. 'Attention please, girls.'

Two hundred heads looked up. 'As you may have noticed, rather a lot of snow has fallen in the night.' Some of the girls laughed but Justice didn't think that the headmistress was in a joking mood. 'It's important that we get the paths clear so that food and other deliveries can get through,' Miss de Vere continued. 'I'm going to divide you into working parties so that we can clear away the snow. I want all you girls to form parties of five. Probably easiest to stay with your dormies. Lessons are cancelled for the morning. There will be hot cocoa in the common room when you come back from your exertions. That's all. Finish your breakfast now.'

'Why do we have to stay with our dormies?' said Rose, going back to her cooling porridge. 'I'd rather be with Alicia.' She looked pointedly at Justice, who smiled innocently back as if she hadn't heard.

'I'd rather not do it at all,' said Eva. 'It'll be freezing. And we've only got our school coats and hats.'

'I don't know why we can't wear trousers,' said Justice. 'It would be much more practical.'

'We can't wear *trousers*,' said Rose. 'We're not *boys*.'

Why not? thought Justice. Mum had told her that women workers had often worn trousers in the war. They were far more practical than skirts. If Justice ever became a headmistress (perish the thought) she would make trousers part of the school uniform.

But when the Barnowls ventured outside, even Rose had to admit that they weren't exactly dressed for the occasion. Within seconds their shoes were soaking and their school raincoats provided very little protection against the bitter wind that was blowing across the marshes. Hutchins had cleared a path through the kitchen garden and issued them with a spade each.

'Got to dig,' he told them, peering out from under his woollen cap. 'Dig a way to the gym.'

'Why?' said Justice, stamping along the path beside Stella. 'Deliveries aren't going to come that way, are they?'

'It's probably so we can do games,' said Rose who, much to her delight, had been allowed to wear her fur hat.

'In that case,' muttered Justice, 'where's our games mistress?'

Outside the garden the snow was a foot deep. They laboured behind Hutchins, taking turns to shovel, but it took them over an hour to get to the outskirts of the gymnasium. Now they were all pink-cheeked and exhausted. Even so, thought Justice, there was something exhilarating about being out in the open. The sun shone on the snow, making it almost unbearably bright, and the sky was a clear, hard blue.

She even enjoyed the shovelling, although she was disappointingly bad at it. Stella was the best, methodical and strong. Justice wondered if she'd been used to doing domestic tasks at home, gardening or bringing in the coal perhaps. The most Justice had had to do was make her bed and water her mother's herb garden. What had happened to the herbs now, she wondered. She couldn't imagine Dad watering them when he got in from court.

Justice jumped as something cold hit her on the back of the neck. She turned and saw Nora grinning at her. Justice grinned back and immediately scooped up some snow and threw it back at her, but Nora ducked and it hit Rose (whoops!) who screamed like a banshee and began pelting Justice with snowballs. Stella jumped in to defend her and before long all the girls were throwing snowballs, laughing as they slipped and slid in their unsuitable shoes.

Hutchins turned. 'Stop that. This is serious. Start digging.'

Why is it serious, thought Justice, feeling a sudden shiver, *if we're just clearing a path to the gym?* But his tone seemed to affect them all, and they took up their spades and began shovelling away again behind the bulky shape of Hutchins.

*   *   *

It wasn't long before the sun and the snow had lost their charm. Justice trudged along, struggling with the heavy spade, trying to widen the path made by Hutchins. It seemed to take for ever, and soon her freezing hands blistered and her back ached. Nora's glasses kept falling off into the snow. Stella worked steadily in front of them. Hutchins didn't turn round again until they reached the gymnasium.

'Well done,' he said to Stella. 'Well tried,' to Justice and Nora. And, 'You two were useless,' to Rose and Eva, who weren't even pretending to help any more. Rose spluttered indignantly and Eva started to say that she had chilblains. Hutchins ignored them both and took a flask from his pocket. He took a swig and handed it to Stella who shook her head. After a pause he handed it to Justice who wiped the top and took a gulp. The liquid tasted like coffee mixed with brandy and it made Justice's head swim. Afterwards, though, it felt as if she had a small heater inside her, warming her right down to the very tips of her toes.

'Thank you,' she said to Hutchins. 'That was super.'

To her surprise, he laughed, showing two missing front teeth. 'Super,' he muttered to himself, looking towards the gymnasium.

Justice followed his gaze. The gym had a roof that jutted out, forming a kind of porch that led all the way round the building. A fine layer of snow had blown on to this area and Justice saw immediately what the handyman was looking at. Footprints. The prints leading to this spot must have been covered by the snow but these had been preserved by the overhanging roof.

'She must have gone that way,' said Hutchins.

'Who?' said Justice, but Hutchins didn't answer. Instead he set off towards the building. Stella and Justice followed, side by side, the others close behind.

They walked around the side of the gymnasium. It was exposed here and the wind whipped the snow into their faces. Justice kept her head down and concentrated on following Hutchins, stepping in the imprints made by his huge boots. It was a bit like Good King Wenceslas, she thought. She approved of the way that Hutchins was avoiding walking over the evidence.

Behind the gym the tower loomed in front of them, its battlements edged in white. Again, beyond the jutting roof of the gym, the footprints stopped and the snow lay smoothly in every direction. Except for a dark space in the near distance.

'What's that?' said Stella.

'It's the old swimming pool,' said Justice, before realising that she shouldn't have known that.

Hutchins showed no sign of having heard her. He walked to the edge of the empty pool and looked down. Justice followed him.

Hutchins turned. 'Stay back!' he shouted. 'Stay back!'

But Justice had reached the pool and looked down. And she had seen the body lying at the bottom, half covered in snow, its neck at an unnatural angle. Miss Thomas. Dead.

CHAPTER 13

Saturday afternoons were normally devoted to sport but, with Miss Thomas unavoidably detained by death, this was obviously impossible. Also the snow had started again. Some of the lower windows were now completely white and Justice heard Hutchins saying that the telephone lines were down. The teachers, who all looked shocked and tearful and – more troubling still perhaps – frightened, didn't seem to know what to do with the two hundred bored and curious girls. In the end, they were corralled into the library where Monsieur Pierre showed slides from France on the magic lantern.

'Let's sneak out,' whispered Justice to Stella. 'If anyone asks us, we can say we're doing prep.'

In fact, no one seemed to notice them go. The first years were all oohing and ahhing at pictures of the Eiffel Tower and the older girls were hoping that they might catch a glimpse of Monsieur Pierre in holiday clothes. There was no sign of Helena and the prefects. Justice thought they had probably gone up to their common room, which was in the attic and actually boasted a wood-burning stove.

Justice and Stella went to the second form common room. Although they didn't have a fire, the room was above the kitchens and so marginally warmer than the rest of the school. Justice and Stella sat on one of the sofas and pulled the rug over them. This was the traditional way of keeping warm and, when the whole form was there, rivalry over the rug could turn quite nasty.

'So,' said Justice. 'Who do you think killed her?'

Stella looked shocked. 'Justice! Miss de Vere said it was an accident.'

Miss de Vere had addressed the girls in the dining hall. She said that Miss Thomas had met with a 'tragic accident' and that they should 'refrain from gossiping about it'. Justice didn't know what they had done with the body.

'They said Mary's death was an accident too,' she said. 'One death looks like misfortune, two looks like carelessness. Oscar Wilde or someone said that.'

'She must have fallen into the pool and broken her neck,' said Stella. 'That's what I heard Matron saying to Miss Crane.'

'Yes, but why was she wandering around the grounds in a snowstorm at night?' said Justice. 'And why was she waiting at the tower that time? You have to admit that it looks suspicious. And I haven't told you what Dorothy told me. She thinks Miss Thomas murdered Mary.'

'Justice! You can't go around saying things like that.'

'It wasn't me! It was Dorothy.' Justice told Stella what Dorothy had said to her about Mary's sickness, and Miss Thomas's visit, and the powder in Mary's drink. By the end, Stella looked positively terrified.

'You've got to tell someone, Justice! Miss de Vere . . . The police . . .'

'Yes, but what if Miss de Vere was involved? She was outside last night. I saw her when I was going to see Dorothy in the attic. She was coming down the attic stairs dressed in her coat and hat. Monsieur Pierre was out of bed too. And Helena Bliss.'

'Helena Bliss? What was *she* doing?'

'Going up to the North Tower in her nightdress by the looks of it.'

'Maybe she was sleepwalking.'

'Maybe, but sleepwalking always seems a bit fishy to me. And Miss de Vere was out and about that night when I went to the tower too. Trust me, *something's* going on in this school.'

'But Miss de Vere's the headmistress. How can she be involved in a murder?'

'You can't tell by appearances,' said Justice, remembering Laura Peruzzi. 'That's what my father always says.'

'Your father!' said Stella. 'You must tell your father. He'll know what to do.' She was obviously desperate to put the whole thing in the hands of a grown-up. But Justice was made of sterner stuff.

'I'll send him our distress code,' she said, 'but it looks as if the post won't get through for a few days. In the meantime, we must conduct our own investigations.'

'But how?' said Stella.

'By applying logic,' said Justice, 'like Sherlock Holmes. Or Leslie Light.'

'But we're not Sherlock Holmes,' said Stella. 'We're just schoolgirls.'

Justice thought her very poor-spirited. She was just about to explain more about Sherlock Holmes' detection methods when the door opened and Miss Morris, the maths teacher, came in.

'I thought I heard voices,' she said. 'What are you doing here, girls?'

'Prep,' said Justice.

'It doesn't look like it. Go back to the hall. Monsieur Pierre has another set of slides to show you.' She sounded as if she wasn't thrilled at the prospect either, so Justice felt brave enough to say, 'What do you think happened to Miss Thomas?'

'She fell into the old pool,' said Miss Morris. 'It was a tragic accident.' Something in the way she said it made Justice think that this was the official line, the phrase the teachers had been told to use.

'But why was she outside at all?'

'She probably went to check on the gymnasium,' said Miss Morris. 'To see if you could do games today.'

There was something wrong with this explanation but Justice couldn't quite put her finger on it, so she said nothing.

'It's such an awful thing to happen,' said Stella, sounding close to tears.

'Don't think too much about it, girls,' said Miss Morris in a softer voice. She still had a shawl clutched around her shoulders and this made her look more approachable than usual, like an old grandmother. But Justice remembered someone saying that Miss Morris had been a pupil at the school. Was she the same age as Miss Thomas?

'Yes, I was at school with Barbara – with Miss Thomas,' said Miss Morris when Justice asked the question.

'You must be very sad then,' said Justice.

Miss Morris gave her a sharp look. 'Yes, I'm very sad,' she said, 'if not exactly surprised. Go back to the hall now.'

In prep they were allowed to write home, but Miss de Vere herself came in to tell them 'not to distress their parents unduly'.

'Just say Miss Thomas met with a tragic accident,' she said.

Those words again, thought Justice.

Eva asked how to spell tragic.

Justice was pretty sure though that even if she did just write to Dad with the 'official line', he would get the message all the same. Mind you, if they were snowed in, there was no way that these letters would ever reach the post. It was worth a try though. Justice wrote:

> Dear Dad,
> There has been a tragic accident and Miss Thomas is dead. Nothing to worry about. Peter's school is giving a concert and Peter is playing the Bach. Can't wait to see him.
> Your loving daughter
> Justice
> P.S. The tuck box is nearly finished. Could you possibly send some more?

That night, in the dormy after lights out, Justice got out her journal once more.

She added a new heading:

THE SECOND MURDER.

Underneath she wrote the now familiar list.

MAIN SUSPECTS — SEEN OUT OF BED AT NIGHT:
1. Miss Thomas (number 1 suspect) — DECEASED
2. Miss de Vere
3. Hutchins
4. Monsieur Pierre
5. Matron
6. Helena Bliss

She sucked her pen for a moment before adding:

7. Miss Morris? (Didn't see her out of bed but she did go to school with Miss Thomas and didn't seem to like her much).

She added another heading.

THE CRIME SCENE

1. *Body found in empty swimming pool. I couldn't see very much (because Hutchins hurried us away) but it looked as if the deceased (Miss Thomas) was lying face down.*
2. *There were footprints under the covered porch. No footprints leading to the gym or by the pool itself because of heavy snowfall.*

She stopped. *That's it!* she thought, suddenly realising what was wrong with Miss Morris's explanation.

Miss Morris had said that Miss Thomas had gone out to check the gymnasium.

But there had been no footsteps in the snow leading to the gym.

Which must mean that Miss Thomas had walked there *before* it had stopped snowing, which it had done by one o'clock when Justice went to bed.

Which must mean that she had gone out into the grounds last night – in the middle of a snowstorm.

Why?

CHAPTER 14

The whole school normally walked across the fields to church on Sundays but the day after Miss Thomas's 'tragic accident' there was no possibility of anyone leaving the building. The snow reached as high as the ground-floor windows and Hutchins was still trying to dig a path to the main gates. At breakfast Miss de Vere announced that, instead, there would be prayers in the assembly hall. She concluded by saying that several servants hadn't been able to get in from the village, so the girls would have to help with clearing away the breakfast things. 'Could I have some volunteers please?'

Justice was the first to put her hand up. If she could find

her way into the kitchen or scullery, there might be a chance of talking to Dorothy.

'Thank you, Justice.' Miss de Vere looked slightly surprised. 'We must all be prepared to help each other through these difficult days.'

The others were quick to follow suit, some waving their hands in the air in an effort to show just how helpful they wanted to be. Miss de Vere allocated tasks and Justice was told to take the dirty plates into the scullery. There she was delighted to find Dorothy, up to her elbows in soapy water.

'Well,' said Justice, dumping down the porridge-encrusted bowls. 'Who do you think killed Miss Thomas?'

Dorothy looked round nervously. 'Miss Thomas fell in the empty pool. That's what Mrs Hopkirk told me.'

'Yes, but what was she doing near the pool in the middle of the night?' said Justice. 'You have to admit that it looks fishy. And, if Miss Thomas is dead, she can't be the person who killed Mary. Unless there are two murderers in the school, of course.'

'Shh!' Dorothy looked round again. 'Someone will hear you.'

'I've made a note of everyone who was out of bed that night,' said Justice. 'I estimate that Miss Thomas fell into the pool – or was pushed – between seven p.m. when the snow started and one a.m. when it had stopped.'

'Please, Justice,' said Dorothy. 'I can't talk about this now.'

'I thought you'd be interested,' said Justice.

'I *am* interested!' whispered Dorothy. 'It's just . . . I'll get in trouble. Can we talk later? In my room, tonight?'

'All right,' said Justice. 'But don't say midnight again.'

At that moment Helena Bliss wafted in carrying a tray piled with plates. 'Shake a leg, Justice,' she said. 'You heard the headmistress. We've all got to pull together and help.'

'Oh, I'm happy to help,' said Justice. Then, feeling slightly daring, she added, 'Any time of the day or night.'

Dorothy gave a little involuntary snort of laughter, which she tried to disguise as a cough.

Helena gave Justice a hard stare, her blue eyes cold as sapphires. 'I'm glad to hear it, Justice. This is about the good of the school, you know.'

'I'm thinking about the good of the school,' said Justice.

'Excellent,' said Helena. 'Then you can go and help Stella with the pigswill.'

Stella was in the lean-to by the kitchens, pouring crusts, porridge and other nameless slime into the pig bins. The snow lay halfway up the glass wall.

'I expect we'll be eating this for lunch tomorrow,' said Stella, wrinkling her nose.

Justice wondered if they'd actually be eating the pigs, which lived in a sty behind the greenhouses. She didn't claim to be an expert on the weather (you didn't really have weather in London, somehow) but the sky was a dull leaden grey and she thought that more snow was likely. How long would they be marooned here on the marshes, with no telephone and no way of communicating with the outside world? The sense of claustrophobia she always felt at Highbury House was growing stronger by the second. She suddenly had a mad impulse to run out into the snow, to keep running until she got to a village, a house, civilisation. *Don't be silly*, she told herself. *We're miles from anywhere. You'd die before you got to a main road.* The thought didn't make her feel comforted exactly.

But Stella must have been thinking along the same lines. 'How long do you think we'll be snowed in?' she said. 'It was fun at first but now . . .'

'I don't know,' said Justice. 'It's a bit worrying that we've got a dead body here and the police don't know anything about it.' She lowered her voice. 'Where do you think they're keeping it . . . the body, I mean?'

'In the ice house,' said Stella. 'I heard Cook saying. Mind you, this whole place is an ice house at the moment. The radiators aren't on. I think they're trying to save on coal.'

Justice had got so used to being cold that she'd hardly noticed that the temperature had dropped. Now she realised that she could see her breath, even indoors.

'I hope the snow stops soon,' said Justice. She seemed to be the only person who realised that there was a killer in the school.

And that the killer might strike again.

When Miss de Vere prayed for Miss Thomas, there were sniffs and sobs all round. Justice watched carefully for signs of guilt. *Never trust a witness who cries in the box.* That's what her dad always said. By that yardstick, most of the girls in the hall were guilty. Eva was in hysterics again and Rose was sobbing picturesquely on Alicia's shoulder. To be fair, though, Rose had seemed to like Miss Thomas and vice versa. And, of course, Rose's mother had been a favourite too. Justice remembered the half-day holiday and the cries of 'Serena!' and 'Tommy!' What would Serena and The Diplomat say when they heard the news? It seemed wrong that the parents still didn't know.

After a half-hearted rendition of 'To Be A Pilgrim', accompanied on the piano by Miss Evans, the music teacher, the younger girls filed out. The upper school remained in the hall where they were going to act Shakespeare scenes with Miss de Vere. This left the lower school to their own devices. They were forbidden to go outside ('for safety reasons', explained Miss de Vere), so everyone traipsed off to the common room.

As she followed behind the others, Justice fretted at the thought of all that evidence – footprints and so on – going to waste, only to be covered by more snow tonight. On the other hand, she didn't feel much like going out in the cold herself. Today the snow did not look sparkly and exciting; it looked sullen and threatening, a great, grey cloak descending on the building and keeping them trapped there.

But she couldn't just sit there and do nothing and wait for someone else to get murdered, could she?

The common room was full by the time she walked in and Rose was holding court from the sofa, the rug draped over her. She doubted anyone would notice if she was there or not.

She was just sneaking back out of the door when she heard a voice behind her.

'What are you doing?'

It was Stella, her head cocked on one side. Justice hadn't really decided until that moment, but she suddenly realised what she had to do.

'I'm going to try to get into Miss de Vere's office,' said Justice. 'It should be safe because she's busy doing *Hamlet* in the hall.'

'Why Miss de Vere's office?' said Stella. For once she didn't sound that shocked. Maybe she was getting used to it, thought Justice. She decided to take the risk and explain.

'Because she's the key to it all. She was going to meet Miss Thomas that night, the first night I went to the tower. And she went out last night too – the night Miss Thomas was murdered.'

The word 'murdered' echoed in the air. They had all got so used to the 'tragic accident' story that the real word sounded shocking, even to Justice.

It seemed to decide Stella though. She squared her shoulders. 'Let's go.'

'Really?' said Justice. 'You don't have to. I wasn't going to ask you. I know how you feel about—'

'Look,' said Stella, interrupting, 'something's obviously going on in this school and you can't search for clues and look out for teachers, so *someone* is going to have to come with you. And besides,' she added with a smile, 'I can't let you and Dorothy have all the fun.'

The school was unnaturally quiet. They took the back stairs up to the corridor with the oil paintings and stuffed animal heads. They could hear the clock ticking in the great hall and the occasional Shakespearean noise from the upper school. Miss de Vere would be busy for at least another hour, thought Justice. Where were the rest of the teachers? Miss Crane, the English mistress, was assisting Miss de Vere, but the others must all be at large. Justice hoped that they were all huddled by the fire in their common room. It was still bitterly cold.

They reached the panelled door to the turret room and, in silence, climbed the spiral stairs. Justice's worst fear was that the office would be closed, but not only was it not locked, the door was slightly ajar. Had Miss de Vere left in a hurry? Justice pushed the door wider and the two girls entered the room.

It looked the same: portraits of departed headmistresses, a cabinet full of trophies, an ornate fireplace (unlit), cold sunlight streaming in through the arched windows.

'What are you looking for anyway?' whispered Stella from her position at the doorway.

'I don't know,' said Justice as she moved over to the desk. She couldn't resist sitting in Miss de Vere's chair, just to see what it felt like to be the headmistress. Powerful, was the answer.

'Justice!' hissed Stella.

There were papers on the desk as well as two books: a copy of Jane Austen's *Persuasion* and a book that Justice knew well because it had been written by her father – *A Short History of Criminal Extortion* by Herbert Jones QC. Justice went to pick it up and, as she did so, dislodged a letter which must have been hidden underneath. She had a moment's qualm about reading the headmistress's private letters, but this was over before she had smoothed the paper open. She wasn't reading it for pleasure, after all. It was almost her *duty*.

The note was typewritten, in capitals.

I KNOW YOUR SECRET. UNLESS YOU WANT ME TO TELL OTHERS MEET ME OUTSIDE THE TOWER AT MIDNIGHT TONIGHT.

Justice's head was swimming. When had this been written? Was this note why Miss de Vere had been out in the grounds that night? Was it from Miss Thomas then – who was also out

151

that night – and, if so, did that mean the games mistress had been blackmailing the headmistress? 'Extortion', as Justice knew well, was a legal term for blackmail. Had Miss de Vere killed Miss Thomas to stop her from telling the world her secret? And what *was* her secret anyway?

Then she noticed that the note had been in an envelope, also typewritten. And the name on the envelope was: Mrs Guy Goddard. Who was this? The name sounded oddly familiar.

'What is it?' whispered Stella. She glanced furtively out of the door, then scurried over, leaving her lookout post.

Justice showed her the note.

'Who wrote this?' said Stella, looking shocked. 'And what's the secret?'

'I don't know,' said Justice. 'It's unsigned.'

Goddard, she was thinking. *Goddard, Goddard, Goddard* . . . Where had she heard that name before? She put the note and the envelope back under the book.

'I'll just have a quick look in the drawers,' she said. 'There might be some clues in here.'

'Well, for goodness sake hurry up,' said Stella. 'She'll be back in a minute.'

'Do not,' said a voice from the doorway, 'refer to your headmistress as *she*.'

CHAPTER 15

Stella started to cry. Justice didn't really blame her, but it wasn't exactly *helpful*.

'Miss de Vere,' she said brightly. 'Fancy seeing you here.'

It wasn't the most tactful of remarks, come to think of it.

'I'm giving you two seconds to think of a reason why you should be in my office,' said Miss de Vere, 'and then I'll be writing to your parents and asking them to remove you from the school.'

Stella sobbed louder. Justice didn't think it was worth reminding Miss de Vere that there wouldn't be any post because of the snow.

'We've got some information,' she said, rather wildly. 'About Miss Thomas's death.' She started to edge out from behind the desk. Miss de Vere swept past her to sit regally in her chair. Justice couldn't help but notice that the headmistress's eyes were drawn to *A Short History of Criminal Extortion*.

Justice stood beside Stella and took hold of her hand.

'I think Miss Thomas was murdered,' she said.

Miss de Vere's eyes were very dark and they seemed to drill into Justice's brain. But Justice couldn't help noticing that the headmistress did not seem exactly shocked at her words.

'You see, I was there when they found the body, and there were no footprints in the snow. That means . . .'

'Enough.' Miss de Vere did not shout but her low voice seemed to reverberate around the room. Justice was sure that she could hear the trophies rattling in the glass-fronted cabinet.

Miss de Vere took a deep breath and seemed to be making up her mind about something. When she spoke again her voice was different, quieter and more measured.

'It's clear you fancy yourself as an amateur sleuth, Justice,' she said. 'That's understandable. After all, your mother wrote crime novels and your father is a criminal barrister. Also, I make allowances for your grief over your mother. Seeing Miss Thomas . . . seeing her like that must have been traumatic for you. For you all.' Her gaze swept over Stella, who was still sniffing.

'But I cannot have girls sneaking around the school trespassing in teachers' private offices. Do you understand?'

'Yes, Miss de Vere,' said Justice.

'Yes, Miss de Vere,' said Stella, wiping her eyes with the back of her hand.

'Miss Thomas's death was a tragic accident. It's an insult to her memory to talk about murder. You will both do extra Latin tonight and miss the rehearsal of the Christmas play.'

Justice had forgotten that there was a rehearsal that evening. Frankly it wasn't much of a punishment to miss seeing Rose and Helena Bliss swanking around in white nightdresses.

'Will you still be writing to our parents?' asked Stella. Her voice was trembling.

'That depends entirely on your behaviour over the next few days,' said Miss de Vere. 'You are dismissed.'

Through some mysterious school semaphore system, by teatime everyone seemed to know about Stella and Justice's disgrace.

'You'll probably be expelled,' said Rose, spreading margarine on her bread (there were already signs that supplies were running low: no butter, no jam, cocoa so weak that it tasted like water). Rose seemed to have recovered from her earlier grief over Miss Thomas. She was wearing her angel costume of white gown and golden wings. Justice thought that she'd wear it all day if she could.

'Oh no.' Eva's eyes filled with tears. 'We would miss you so much.'

'We'd miss Stella,' said Rose.

'We'd miss *both* of them,' said Nora. Justice was rather touched.

'We won't get expelled,' Justice said. 'Miss de Vere wasn't even that angry.'

'She was,' said Stella. She had been very subdued since the encounter in Miss de Vere's office.

'You'll miss the rehearsal,' said Rose.

'I know,' said Justice. 'That's the worst punishment ever.'

Rose eyed her narrowly. She never seemed entirely sure when Justice was being sarcastic. She contented herself with saying, 'It'll be cold all alone in the prep room. You'll freeze.'

This last bit was probably true. After tea, Justice decided to sneak up to the common room and borrow the rug to put over their feet. The great hall was deserted. She ran quickly up the main stairs and started along the first-floor corridor. Then she froze. At the end of the corridor she could see Helena Bliss, wearing a white gown, wings and a large golden halo, coming the other way. She was accompanied by Davina, her angel-in-waiting friend, similarly dressed but without the halo. Justice darted quickly behind a suit of armour.

'I'm going to the North Turret at midnight tonight,' Helena was saying. 'He'll be there.'

'Oh, Helena,' said Davina. 'Be careful.'

They clattered down the stairs, their school shoes looking odd beneath the angel dresses. Justice stayed hidden, breathing rather fast.

Why was Helena going to the North Turret at midnight? And who was 'he'?

There was only one way to find out.

CHAPTER 16

Rex v Stanley.

Rex v Donagh and West.

Rex v Hamilton.

Rex v Pewsey.

Justice lay in bed going through old murder trials again, trying to keep herself awake till she could be sure everyone else was asleep. She was going to do this. She was going to find out what Helena Bliss was doing when she wandered about the school at night. She would call in on Dorothy too. She could do with another brain on the case and after their encounter with Miss de Vere, Stella would be too scared to break any more rules. And if she, Justice, got expelled, well . . . at least she'd get to escape from Highbury House and go home. And wasn't that what she wanted anyway? But, even as she thought this, she realised that there were people she'd miss about the school. Stella and Dorothy, of course, but also Nora and Eva. Even Rose in a way . . .

Rex v Hughes.

Rex v Bayliss and Bayliss.

Rex v Peruzzi.

Rex v Goddard.

It wasn't really that difficult staying awake because her mind was buzzing.

Who was Helena Bliss meeting in the North Turret at midnight? Who was blackmailing Miss de Vere, and why? Who pushed Miss Thomas into the empty swimming pool? Who killed Mary?

Gradually the dormy fell silent. Outside an owl hooted. Under the covers, Justice switched on her torch and looked at her watch. Half past eleven. She got up and tiptoed to the door, then stood in the corridor for a moment, listening. The school was eerily quiet tonight. No footsteps, no doors opening and shutting, no whispered conversations. It was so quiet that you could hear the grandfather clock ticking in the hall, two floors below.

Justice crept along the landing and gently opened the door that led to the attic stairs. She stood still, listening. Nothing. Just the creaks and groans of an old house at night; floorboards expanding, mice scurrying along skirting boards (Rudi, Mrs Hopkirk's cat, was far too fat and lazy to catch mice). Justice climbed the stairs to the attic. The door to the North Turret was open. Would she find Helena in there? Justice edged nearer until she could see into the room. At first, she thought it was empty and then she saw a figure lying on the floor. A girl with long blonde hair.

Helena Bliss.

Justice didn't know that she had screamed but she must have done because, after a few seconds, Dorothy came running into the room.

'What is it? Justice! What are yo— Oh my God! Is that...? Is she...?'

'It's Helena,' said Justice, barely able to get her words out. 'I think she's dead. Stay here while I get Miss de Vere.'

'Stay here?' said Dorothy. 'Not likely.' She followed Justice back along the corridor and down the stairs. On the dormitory landing, Justice paused. She was near the door to the teachers' living quarters but they were so strictly out of bounds that, even now, she hesitated. While she waited, though, the door opened and Miss de Vere came out. Fully dressed, Justice couldn't help noticing.

'Justice! What are you doing here? What was that noise?'

After a few seconds they were joined by Monsieur Pierre in a purple velvet dressing gown. And by Matron wearing something pink and quilted.

'What are you doing out of bed, Justice?' asked Matron as soon as she saw her. 'You'll receive an order mark for this.'

'It's Helena,' said Justice. 'She's lying on the floor. I think she's dead.'

Monsieur Pierre let out a strange Gallic curse and Matron put her hand on her heart, but Miss de Vere just said, 'Where?'

'In the turret room.'

Justice, Dorothy, Matron and Monsieur Pierre followed Miss de Vere along the corridor. When they came to the door, though, Justice stopped, suddenly afraid to go inside. She heard Miss de Vere say, 'Oh no,' and Monsieur Pierre muttering what sounded like a prayer. Dorothy clung to Justice's arm, sobbing quietly.

Matron was leaning over Helena's body. She straightened up. 'We need to get her to sickbay at once, Dolores.' It took

Justice a few seconds before she realised that Matron was addressing Miss de Vere. She'd forgotten that her name was Dolores. She heard Miss de Vere take a deep breath before she spoke. 'Justice, Dorothy. Go to Dorothy's room and wait for me there. Jean-Maurice, Evelyn, I need you to help me with . . . with Helena.'

Justice didn't want to see any more. She grabbed Dorothy's arm and propelled her along the corridor.

In Dorothy's room they sat on the bed in silence, holding hands. After a while, though, they were so cold that they got under the covers.

'Was she dead?' said Dorothy at last. 'Did you see?'

'I don't know,' said Justice. 'I couldn't see her breathing.'

'But who would murder Helena? Everyone loved her.'

Not everyone, thought Justice. But she kept that thought to herself.

After a few minutes, Miss de Vere came into the room. The headmistress looked very pale but otherwise she was completely composed. She could have been about to preside over a morning assembly.

Miss de Vere sat on the chair by Dorothy's bed. The two girls looked at her without speaking. Miss de Vere brushed down her skirt, smoothing the tweed with her fingertips. Justice noticed her hands for the first time. They were surprisingly big for such a slender woman. They looked strong.

'We've taken Helena to sickbay,' said Miss de Vere in a low voice. 'Matron is looking after her now.'

'Is she dead?' whispered Dorothy.

'No,' said Miss de Vere, but she didn't meet their eyes. Justice wondered if she was lying. 'But she's very sick. Now girls, I want to ask you something very important. You see, we're in a very difficult position now. The phone lines are still down and the school is completely cut off by the snow. I can't get hold of a doctor . . .'

'Or the police,' Justice couldn't help saying.

Miss de Vere leant forward. Her eyes glittered in the dim light. 'I know you fancy yourself a detective, Justice, but I must ask you not to let your imagination run away with you. Miss Thomas's death was a tragic accident. Helena has simply suddenly . . . become very ill.'

'She looked like she was dead,' said Justice.

'You must never say that,' said Miss de Vere, speaking quietly but with deadly emphasis. 'The last thing we want is to cause panic and hysteria. You're a *schoolgirl* and these are *adult* matters. You can't possibly understand what's going on. You must leave everything in my hands. You must promise to say nothing about this to anyone. Do you understand? From now on, everyone must also stay in their dormitories after lights out,' continued the headmistress. 'I want your word on that, Justice. I can't have you wandering around on your own at night. You'll be safe if you stick with the other girls. Do you agree?'

Justice and Dorothy nodded wordlessly. What else could they do? But Justice noted that Miss de Vere did not explain what had happened to make Helena 'very ill'. Was it the same thing that had killed Mary?

CHAPTER 17

There was consternation when Helena Bliss did not say Grace at breakfast the next day.

'Where's Helena?' said Nora. 'She's never missed breakfast before.'

'Perhaps she's ill,' said Eva. 'We must make her a get-well card.'

'I'll ask Davina,' said Rose. 'She's sure to know.'

Rose got up and went to the prefects' table. It was a measure of how informal things had become that this daring behaviour went unchallenged. It was true that Rose had always been able to get away with flouting rules, but the school seemed to have become a different place in the last few days. Justice had to admit that she had actually preferred it before. At least then there had been a structure, something to rebel against. Now she had the uneasy feeling that no one really knew what to do next and the headmistress, the person who was supposed to be in charge, was at best completely at a loss and, at worst, a murderer.

Rose came back to the Barnowl table looking important.

'Helena is ill. Davina says that Miss de Vere came into the sixth-form dormy and told them. She's in sickbay.'

'Maybe she's got what Mary had,' said Eva.

You can say that again, thought Justice. She was finding the whole secret thing a bit of a strain. She desperately wanted to tell Stella about last night but she had promised and, besides, Stella had been scared enough when Justice had suggested that Miss Thomas had been murdered. What would she say if she knew that Helena Bliss was lying in sickbay, very ill or perhaps even dead? Miss de Vere had been right about the hysteria, if nothing else. Justice dreaded to think what would happen if the other girls knew. There would be screaming, crying, fainting, total panic. She thought again about the first time she had met Miss de Vere and the headmistress's warning about boarding school life – *Boarding school can be difficult, everyone cooped up together all the time, especially in an isolated place like this. Tensions can rise, tempers can flare unexpectedly, words get spoken that cannot easily be revoked.*

The words now seemed to have acquired a sinister tinge. Was this what had happened with Helena? Had she said something that couldn't be revoked? Something that had led to her being killed?

'Are you all right, Justice?' said Stella.

'I'm fine,' said Justice. 'Just a headache.'

Actually, she did have a headache. All those disturbed nights were finally catching up with her. In Latin, even Miss Bathurst, who could hardly see more than two inches in front of her, noticed that something was wrong.

'Are you all right, Justice?' The teacher peered at her. 'You look very pale.'

'Just a headache,' said Justice again.

'I can't send you to sickbay,' said Miss Bathurst, 'because Helena's in there and Miss de Vere says she might be contagious. But why don't you go to the common room and read quietly? You're so far ahead in this subject anyway.'

Justice didn't need to be told twice. Ignoring Rose's whispers of 'not fair', she gathered up her things and set off for the common room. The school was quiet, everyone was in lessons, and outside the snow lay like a great smothering blanket on the countryside. Justice looked out of one of the staircase windows. The upper field was completely white. Funny how the snow made everything look different. The gymnasium had icicles hanging like Christmas decorations; the tower had become a fairy-tale castle. As she watched, she saw a figure moving towards the gym, tunnelling its way through the snow. Hutchins in a heavy coat and furry hat. What was he doing? Surely all his energies ought to be directed on making a path through the lower field to the outside world? Hutchins stopped as if exhausted and Justice saw him looking up towards the school. Although she was pretty sure that he couldn't see her, she ducked below the sill. When she straightened up, Hutchins had disappeared. Where had he gone? Had she only imagined him?

Justice took the maids' stairs to the common room but she didn't go inside. Instead, she continued up to the attic. Dorothy hadn't been at breakfast. Maybe, she too was feeling under strain. In any case, Justice needed to talk to her. She raced up the stone stairs, hardly caring if she met anyone coming down.

Dorothy's door was open. Her bed was neatly made and there was a note lying on it.

Dear Miss de Vere,
I can't keep working here any more. I'm too scared. I've gone home to my mum.
Sorry.
Dorothy

Justice stood still in the attic bedroom. She felt as if her heart had turned to ice. She must be one of the few people in the school who knew Dorothy's handwriting and so she was absolutely positive about one thing.

Dorothy hadn't written this note.

CHAPTER 18

There was nothing for it now but to take Stella into her confidence. Justice still didn't trust Miss de Vere enough to tell her that Dorothy hadn't written the letter. Dorothy was in danger and Justice didn't think that she could save her on her own. She needed an ally and Stella was the only friend she could truly rely on. When Stella came out of Latin, laughing with Nora as if she hadn't a care in the world, Justice was waiting outside.

'I've got to talk to you,' she said, grabbing her arm and steering her to one side.

Stella looked serious immediately. 'What is it?'

Justice waited for the other girls to stream past, giggling and wondering what was for lunch. (Justice never understood why the girls speculated about this as all the meals were equally horrid.)

'I've got something to tell you,' she said. 'You mustn't scream.'

Stella didn't make a sound when Justice told her about Helena being found in the turret room, but she did go white as a sheet and put her hand over her mouth.

'That's horrible,' she said when she eventually removed the hand. 'Why hasn't Miss de Vere told us?'

'Because we're snowed in and she doesn't want everyone to panic,' said Justice. 'Dorothy knows but I've just gone up to her room and there was a letter on her bed saying that she's scared and she's gone home to her mum.'

'I don't blame her,' said Stella. 'I wish I could go home to my mum.'

'The point is, Dorothy didn't write that letter,' said Justice. 'I know her handwriting from the note she sent me. This was completely different. I think someone has taken Dorothy.'

'Taken her?'

'Kidnapped her. Maybe even . . .'

'Justice.' Stella clutched her arm. 'We've got to tell Miss de Vere.'

'We can't,' said Justice. 'There's still a chance that Miss de Vere is the murderer. We already know she was being

174

blackmailed and that she's been sneaking around the school at night. We just can't trust her.'

'I can't believe that,' said Stella, her face crumpling. 'She's the headmistress . . .' She tailed off as if even she was now unconvinced.

'Look,' said Justice. 'We have to find Dorothy. We have to find her and catch the killer. Before someone else dies.'

'How can we catch the killer?' said Stella. 'We're just schoolgirls. We don't know anything about catching murderers. An adult should be in charge.'

'There isn't an adult we can trust,' said Justice briskly. 'And besides, I've read a lot of crime novels. As Leslie Light always says, "Assemble the facts and look for a pattern." All the clues are here. I just have to work out the pattern. In the meantime, we have to find Dorothy. There's so much snow outside. She can't have got far, so she must be in the school somewhere.'

'But where?' said Stella.

'That's where you can help,' said Justice. 'You've been here for five years. I've made a plan of the school but I don't know all the hiding places.'

'I don't know much either,' said Stella. 'A lot of the school is out of bounds – the teachers' rooms, the basement, the attic, the servants' quarters . . .'

'Well, those are the places to start, then,' said Justice. 'I'll go on having a headache this afternoon. You find some reason to get out of maths. We'll search the whole school if we have to.'

'Shall we start now?' said Stella.

Justice smiled. 'No. We should have lunch. We'll need our strength.'

Justice managed to eat her lunch. It was shepherd's pie and tasted as if it were made of actual shepherds.

'Is your headache still bad?' asked Eva sympathetically.

'Yes,' said Justice. 'I don't think I'll go back to classes this afternoon. I'll just sit quietly in the common room.'

'You won't be allowed to,' said Rose.

But Justice was pretty sure that no one would complain. The teachers were all so distracted that they might not even notice her absence.

'I feel a bit ill too,' said Stella. Justice thought that her acting skills were very poor, but the other girls didn't seem to notice and all made sympathetic noises.

'And Helena's obviously still poorly,' said Nora, pointing towards the prefects' table. Justice and Stella avoided looking at each other. 'I hope we don't all catch whatever it is.'

'So do I,' said Justice.

*   *   *

The first lesson in the afternoon was maths. Justice asked to be excused and Miss Morris made no objection, simply giving her some sums 'to take your mind off your headache'. Justice headed towards the common room where she was joined a few minutes later by Stella.

'I said I was feeling sick,' said Stella, 'and Miss Morris said that it must have been the shepherd's pie.'

Justice thought of the pig bins. 'She's probably right. Now, here's my plan of the house'. She got out her map, the one she had started on her very first day at Highbury House. 'Dorothy won't be in any of the classrooms or dormitories. I think our best bets are the attic or the basement. And the outhouses, of course.' She waited for Stella to say that these areas were out of bounds.

But she had misjudged her friend. 'We should go now,' she said. 'We've got an hour until afternoon recess. Shall we split up?'

But Miss de Vere's words were echoing in Justice's head. *You'll be safe if you stick with the other girls.*

'We'd better stay together,' she said. 'Let's start with the basement. That's the most likely because no one goes there. The music rooms and sixth-form common room are in the attic.'

The basements were reached by a door next to the kitchen. Justice and Stella stood in the corridor listening to the sounds of washing up. Cook must be doing it herself because Ada, the scullery maid, came in from the village. And there was no Dorothy.

'Now,' said Justice, as a loud clatter came from the sinks.

They ran for the door and headed down the dark stone stairs.

'Is there any electricity down here?' said Stella as they groped their way to the bottom.

'I don't think so,' said Justice, 'but I've got my torch.' She switched it on and the wavering beam picked out a brick ceiling, curved walls, a stone floor.

'I don't think anyone comes down here,' said Stella.

'I think they do,' said Justice. 'Look at the floor. No dust. And that door opened pretty easily. I think someone came here fairly recently.'

This was actually a rather frightening thought. Justice found herself standing a little closer to Stella.

'Let's start searching,' she said, trying to sound brave.

Justice shone her torch carefully along the walls but there were no other doors, just the occasional alcove, some full of barrels. Justice wondered what was in them as Cook only ever seemed to make meat pies and tapioca pudding (and dead baby, of course). The passage went straight for a while, then turned sharply left and then right. Justice had almost given up trying to work out which part of the school was above them. They moved slowly, staying close together. If someone had followed them, Justice couldn't help thinking, there would be nowhere to hide.

Eventually the passage came to an end. In front of them was another staircase with a door on either side of it. Justice tried one of the doors. It was locked. 'Dorothy?' she called. Her voice echoed against the low ceiling. 'Dorothy? Dorothy? Dorothy?'

To her surprise, the other door opened easily, and they found themselves in a small room. Justice shone her torch and it picked out some strange apparatus that looked like boxes with dials and wires attached.

She turned to Stella. 'What's that?'

'I don't know,' said Stella. 'Something electrical?'

Justice suddenly remembered something. The room they had hidden in when she had told Stella about Miss de Vere's pen. The storeroom below the North Turret. There had been boxes there labelled 'Electrical equipment. Do not touch'. Justice and Stella had actually used them as chairs. What *was* this mysterious electrical equipment? And could it be linked to the murders? 'Let's keep searching,' said Justice. 'I wonder where this staircase goes?'

'Oh, don't go up it, Justice,' begged Stella. 'Let's go back the way we came.'

But Justice had almost got to the door at the top. It opened easily and she stepped into a large room. The light was very bright after the basement, almost blue. It was a few seconds before Justice realised that this was the snow, visible through several large windows.

'Stella,' she hissed. 'We're in the assembly hall.'

'Thank goodness,' said Stella, appearing beside her. 'Let's hurry up and get somewhere we're allowed to be.'

'Shh,' said Justice. 'Someone's coming.'

Stella gave a soft moan.

'Quick! Behind the stage curtain.'

They climbed on to the stage and concealed themselves behind the blue velvet curtains.

They were only just in time. Two people entered the hall carrying a large box between them. They walked quickly across the room, opened the door to the basement and disappeared.

Justice and Stella looked at each other from within the folds of the curtain.

'Miss de Vere and Monsieur Pierre,' breathed Stella.

'Yes,' said Justice. *And what was in the box?*

CHAPTER 19

'Let's follow them,' said Justice.

'We can't,' said Stella. 'They'd see us. We'll have to go back later.'

They stood in the blue shadow of the stage curtains, staring at each other. The adventure seemed to be getting bigger and more dangerous with every minute.

'Do you think it was . . . do you think it was Dorothy in the box?' whispered Stella, wide-eyed. 'Her body, I mean . . .' She looked horrified at herself for even saying the words.

'I don't know,' said Justice. 'But the box didn't look heavy enough to me. They seemed to be carrying it quite

181

easily. Anyway, it proves they're in it together. Miss de Vere and Monsieur Pierre.'

'In what?' said Stella. 'Do you really think they killed Dorothy? And Miss Thomas? And Helena? And Mary?' Her voice rose.

'Well, they're certainly doing something furtive,' said Justice.

'What do we do now?' said Stella.

'Let's check the attic,' said Justice. 'I didn't have a proper look when I went up earlier. I just came straight back down to find you. There might be some clues up there.'

'It's nearly time for afternoon recess,' said Stella. 'We'd better hurry.'

The great hall was still silent. They took the main stairs, past the suits of armour and the gloomy oil paintings, which now all seemed to be staring at them out of their painted eyes. Justice thought of Hutchins shovelling snow earlier, of the headmistress's face when she'd asked them to keep the secret about Helena. Was there anyone in the school that they could trust?

As they made it up the stairs to the first landing, they heard a voice behind them.

'Where, may I ask, are you going?' It was Miss Morris, the maths mistress, carrying a pile of exercise books.

'To the dormy,' improvised Justice wildly. 'I've got a headache.'

'The dormies are out of bounds during the day, as you well know. Aren't you girls in enough trouble?'

Did Miss Morris know about Justice and Stella being caught in Miss de Vere's office or was she referring to something else? Justice could sense Stella shrinking behind her.

Miss Morris stared at them. Her eyes were small and bright behind her glasses. 'Go back downstairs at once,' she said at last. 'It's nearly recess and we're letting you girls go out into the courtyard. Hutchins has cleared away most of the snow. I'm sure a bit of fresh air will do you all the good in the world. It might even stop you getting these headaches, Justice.'

In the courtyard they met Rose, Nora and Eva glumly walking around with the others. The snow had all been heaped into the middle, leaving a narrow path around the outside. Some of the girls were throwing snowballs but mostly they were just walking with their heads down. It reminded Justice of illustrations she had seen of inmates exercising in prison.

'Feeling better?' said Rose with heavy irony.

'Yes, thanks,' said Justice, who knew that it annoyed Rose when she took this sort of remark at face value. 'Very kind of you to ask.'

'Isn't it horrible?' said Eva, kicking at an icy clod of snow. 'I wish it would all melt and we could get back to normal life.'

It would take more than a thaw to get this school back to normal, thought Justice. Aloud she said, 'Do you know if Hutchins has cleared a path to the gate?'

'He was out there this morning,' said Nora, 'but I heard someone saying that all the roads are still blocked. There's no way off the marsh.'

There's no way off the marsh. Justice thought of the first time she had seen the school, the way the building with its dark turrets had risen above the flat fields all round it. She also remembered what she'd written in her journal. *'Chance of escape without being seen: minimal.'*

In prep, Justice worked out her plan of action. The other second formers were whispering together or working half-heartedly. Eva was making a get-well card for Helena. Eva was rather good at art and was famous for her cartoons. She'd done one of Justice in a toga declaiming Latin. Justice had pinned it on the wall above her bed but

Matron had taken it down. Now Eva was drawing Helena as an angel, which struck Justice as being all too appropriate.

She got out her journal.

MAIN SUSPECTS – SEEN OUT OF BED AT NIGHT:
1. Miss Thomas (number 1 suspect) – DECEASED
2. Miss de Vere
3. Hutchins
4. Monsieur Pierre
5. Matron
6. Helena Bliss
7. Miss Morris (Didn't see her out of bed but she did go to school with Miss Thomas and didn't seem to like her much).

She put a ring round Miss de Vere's name and Monsieur Pierre's and wrote:

Carrying a large box. Suspicious?

Then on a separate page she wrote in big letters:

DOROTHY. Where is she???
1. Attics? I looked in her bedroom but she could be somewhere else on that floor. The sixth form common room? Music practice rooms?

2. *Sickbay. It's out-of-bounds because Helena might be 'contagious' (query: dead?). Could Dorothy be there too?*
3. *Basements — searched. Unless D was in the box. Don't think this!*
4. *The Teachers' Quarters. Safe because completely o-of-b. Could Miss de V have hidden Dorothy there?*
5. *Outhouses. There are so many of them and only Hutchins has the keys. Why was Hutchins in the grounds just now???*
6. *The Tower???*

Justice shut her journal in frustration. She just kept coming back to the same thing. If the roads across the marsh were still impassable, then Dorothy *must* be in the building or in the grounds somewhere. There was nothing else for it; Justice would have to ignore her promise to Miss de Vere and go out again that night.

The dormy was as freezing as ever. Justice tried to get into her pyjamas as quickly as possible, without ever once exposing any skin. The other Barnowls were performing similar contortions around the room. While Rose was in the bathroom, Justice waited by the far window and looked out over the school grounds. There was a full moon, just like the night when she'd first gone out to meet Dorothy, and she could see the grounds laid out quite clearly. Her heart stopped. A path had been cleared to the tower. *Who could have done that, and why?*

186

The snow was silver and the tower dark against the cloudy sky. She remembered the first time she'd seen it and the odd glimmer from the narrow windows. And there it was again. It must be a reflection of the moon. But no, there seemed to be a pattern to it this time.

Yes! There it was again. Three short flashes and three long, then three short again. Justice stood watching, her heart thumping.

Dot, dot, dot. Dash, dash, dash. Again and again.

There was no doubting it now. Someone in the tower was making the Morse code signal for SOS.

Save our souls.

CHAPTER 20

When she came out of the bathroom Justice asked Stella to help French braid her hair. They were allowed to have their hair loose at night, but Justice liked to keep hers tied back to stop it getting too knotty. Stella, having younger sisters, was excellent at hair and was in great demand as a plaiter. So no one thought it odd when Justice and Stella went to the far end of the room where the light was better. They sat on the floor below the single light bulb.

'You've got lovely hair, Justice,' said Stella, brushing it gently.

'Thanks,' said Justice. She lowered her voice. 'I'm going to the tower tonight.'

'What?' Stella let the brush fall with a clatter. Eva and Nora, who were having a half-hearted row about towels, looked round. Rose was already in bed.

Justice waited until Eva and Nora had started up again. 'I saw someone signalling from the tower,' she said quietly. 'I think it was Dorothy. I'm going to find out.'

'You can't! Anyway, you'll never get through the snow.'

'Someone's cleared a path there. You can see it through the window.'

Stella sighed and started braiding again. 'Do you want me to go with you?' she whispered.

Justice was touched. She knew that, for some unknown reason, Stella didn't enjoy this sort of thing. Dorothy would have been far keener but, of course, it was Dorothy who now needed rescuing. 'No,' she said. 'I think it's better if you stay here. I just want you to know. In case . . . well, just in case.'

'I wish you weren't going,' muttered Stella.

'I'll be fine,' said Justice.

'You're very brave,' said Stella, and finishing her braids with a tie at the end, she gave Justice's arm a squeeze. It helped. A lot.

Justice was so tired that it was hard to keep awake. The murder trials kept swimming round in her head and getting confused with other words and phrases, hazy and half-remembered.

Words get spoken that cannot easily be revoked.

There's no way off the marsh.

Chance of escape without being seen: minimal.

Meet me at the tower at midnight.

In the tower no one could hear her scream.

She told Rose to be careful because there was a murderer in the school.

Veritas et fortitudo.

Will you keep our secret?

There's no way off the marsh.

She couldn't wait until midnight. Dorothy was in danger – she had to get out there as soon as possible. She thought of Nora's ghost story, Grace Highbury dying in the tower with no one to rescue her. Well, that wouldn't happen to Dorothy.

When the room was full of regular breathing, supplemented by Eva's familiar squeaks, Justice sat up and slid quietly out of bed. She put on her coat, which was still hidden in her bedside locker, pulled on thick socks and carried her shoes in one hand and her torch in the other. She tiptoed past the sleeping girls, trying to make no sound. She was nearly at the door when an angry voice broke the silence.

'What do you think you're doing?'

Justice turned. Hell's bells and buckets of blood. It was Rose.

Rose's voice was low, so as not to attract the attention of passing teachers, but it was sharp enough to rouse the other Barnowls. Rose turned on the light and all the girls sat up in their beds, rubbing their eyes.

'What's happening?' came Eva's voice. 'Is someone else dead?'

'No one's dead,' said Justice. 'I'm just going out for a walk.'

'At this hour?' said Rose. 'I don't think so.' Justice heard Rose searching for something in her locker, then blinked in the sudden light of a torch.

'Come on,' said Rose, her voice hard and disconcertingly adult. 'Out with it.'

Justice took a deep breath. 'I think someone is being held prisoner in the tower.'

Eva gave a muffled scream.

A loud *ssshhh* came from the other beds.

'A prisoner?' said Rose. 'You've been listening to too many of Nora's ghost stories.'

'Look,' said Justice, trying to sound reasonable. 'I know it sounds mad, but I think Dorothy is being held prisoner in the tower. I think it's because she knows something about Miss Thomas's death.'

'Miss Thomas fell into the old pool,' said Rose. 'It was an accident.'

'No,' said Justice. 'It wasn't.'

There was a silence, and then Stella said, from the far end of the room, 'It's true, Rose. Justice has been finding things out. Awful things have been going on.'

'She's brainwashed you,' said Rose, still in that hard, flat voice. 'She's turned your head. You used to be a normal schoolgirl before Justice came along, thinking she's so clever, thinking she knows everything, thinking that school and games and all the normal things are just *so* boring. Highbury House used to be a super place until she came along and now . . .' Suddenly the adult voice vanished and Rose sobbed like a child. 'Now everything's ruined.'

Eva jumped out of bed to comfort Rose, always the default reaction of any of the Barnowls, but Nora looked across at Justice and, with a serious note that made Justice remember that she was one of the cleverest girls in the form, said, 'Is this true, Justice? Do you really think that Dorothy is locked in the tower? It's not just a silly game?'

Justice could feel the opinions in the room, as finely weighted as the scales of justice themselves, shifting. Would the group decide in favour of her, the new girl, or Rose, the dormy captain and acknowledged leader of the second form? Before Justice could answer, Stella said, 'It's true. I didn't want to believe it. You know me. I haven't got a wild imagination and I hate drama. But terrible things are happening in this school and I think that Justice is right about Dorothy.'

Justice could feel the balance moving in her favour. Stella was much respected by the other girls for her calmness and rationality. But then Rose said, 'In that case, I'm calling a teacher. We can't possibly deal with this sort of thing on our own.' She got up and walked to the door. Justice jumped in front of her.

'No. We can't. We don't know if the teachers are involved.'

Now the room was completely silent. Rose and Justice stared at each other. Rose's blue eyes were cold and yet Justice thought she could sense something else going on inside. Was it fear? Anger? Understanding?

There was a movement among the girls and Stella came to stand next to Justice by the door.

'I'll come with you,' she said.

Justice felt her eyes prickle. She knew what this would have cost Stella, to stand up to Rose, to offer to break yet more school rules, to walk into potential danger.

'It's OK,' she said. 'I need you here to keep watch. Look.' She turned to Rose, trying to sound sensible and friendly, trying to sound, in fact, like that fabled creature, the normal schoolgirl. 'Give me an hour. If I'm not back then, you can alert Matron. How about that?'

Rose continued to stare at her. The other Barnowls watched in silence as, slowly, Rose moved away from the door.

It was very cold outside. The wind was whipping up the snow so that it flew in Justice's face as she made her way round the school towards the gymnasium and the tower. But Hutchins had done his work well. There was definitely a path and it wasn't too hard to follow. At times the snow was almost at waist height on either side of her. It was like pictures she had seen of toboggan runs in Switzerland. Justice walked quickly. She only had an hour. Just one hour to save Dorothy and bring her back to the school before the teachers would be alerted. You could be sure that Rose would raise the alarm as soon as the sixty minutes was up. Justice walked faster and faster, her jagged breathing amplified by the snow tunnel. She had to get to the tower. She wouldn't think about what would come next.

Veritas et fortitudo, she told herself. Truth and courage. That was all that mattered.

Past the gymnasium and the old pool, the path veered to the right, through the trees towards the tower. This, to Justice, was further proof that Dorothy was imprisoned there. She wondered who had cleared the path. She had seen Hutchins out there today. Could it have been him all along? Why, otherwise, would he have tunnelled through the snow like this? She thought of the handyman, his height, his strength, and hoped that Hutchins wouldn't be waiting for her at the tower. He would overpower her in seconds. But Dorothy wouldn't have signalled if the coast wasn't clear. She trudged on, head down against the swirling snow.

For a moment, she was under the cover of the trees, then suddenly – the tower was there. The ramparts were edged in white but the snow hadn't stuck to its sleek black walls. The full moon hung in the sky behind it, like an illustration on one of the tarot cards Mum's friend Lois used to read. And there was the door in front of her, looking very shut indeed. Justice tried the handle. But it was locked.

Justice stamped at the ground in frustration. She realised that she hadn't given a thought as to how she would get into the tower once she had reached it. She rattled the doorknob again and again. It was definitely locked. But, on the path at her feet, there was a muddle of footprints. Proof that someone – several someones – had been this way recently.

'Dorothy!' Justice shouted in desperation. 'Dorothy! Are you there?'

And, to her amazement, a voice answered.

'Justice? Is that you?'

Justice looked up. Dorothy's pale face was just visible in one of the narrow windows. It was like a fairy story, thought Justice. The princess in the tower. But, in this case, the rescuer had come up against a firmly bolted door. Justice bit her lip in frustration. It was ridiculous to have got this far and not be able to get inside. What had happened in the story? The princess had thrown down her hair and the prince had climbed up it, or some such nonsense. But neither Dorothy nor Justice would fit through that window even if there had been a handy hair ladder.

'Dorothy! Are you all right?' Justice's voice echoed in the still night air. She hoped that Dorothy's abductor was not in earshot.

'I'm locked in.' Dorothy's voice floated down to her. 'I got a note – I thought it was from you – saying to meet you by the tower.'

Dorothy sounded upset at being fooled in this way, but Justice knew that, in the circumstances, she would have done exactly the same thing. After all, she had come to the tower at midnight that first time, not knowing who she was going to meet.

'I'm going to get help,' she said. 'Stay here,' she added, somewhat unnecessarily.

But as she went to turn, something struck her on the head.

Darkness descended.

CHAPTER 21

Justice was sitting with Mum under a tree, dappled light was shining through the branches and Mum was telling her a story about a princess locked in a tower.

She was walking along a beach with Dad, the waves breaking against the stones. 'Shallow seas,' Dad was saying. 'There must be hundreds of shipwrecks out there.'

She was running across the marshes, knowing that something was behind her, something unknown but terrifying, something that was gaining on her with every second.

There's no way off the marsh.

'Justice!'

She opened her eyes but the darkness was still all around. Then she saw a pale face looking down at her. Who was it? There was a flash of white and a smell, mustiness mixed with something surgical and clean. Then a smile, orange gums . . .

'Don't worry, you're safe now.'

Oh, thank goodness. It was Matron. She'd never felt so pleased to see that white nurse's uniform. Was she back at the school in sickbay? No, she could see the stone walls of the tower, the rafters high up in the roof, the tiny slits of windows.

'You hit your head,' Matron was saying. 'I saw you creeping out of the school and followed you. You're in big trouble, young lady.'

Justice had heard this so often that it was almost soothing.

'Where's Dorothy?' she said. 'She was locked in the tower . . .'

'She's here. I don't know what silly prank you two were playing but it will probably cost Dorothy her job. I'll have to tell Miss de Vere about this.'

'No!' said Justice. 'Please . . .'

'Please don't!' Dorothy's voice came from the darkness. 'I only came here because I got a note . . .'

'All this silliness about notes and secret signals,' said Matron. 'Aren't things bad enough at the school already?

Now, I've got to get help. You shouldn't move, Justice. I think you've got concussion. Stay here while I go back to the school.'

Stay here. That's what Justice had said to Dorothy. Silly. What else could they do? The little bit of sky that she could see through the windows was jet black. It was still the middle of the night.

'Don't leave us here,' said Dorothy.

'Don't be ridiculous. There's nothing to be afraid of.'

'But what about the ghost . . .' said Dorothy, who had obviously heard the Grace Highbury story.

'Stuff and nonsense,' said Matron. 'You stay here quietly and I'll go for Miss de Vere and Hutchins. You need to be moved to sickbay, Justice. I've brought you some herbal tea.' She gestured to a tartan thermos flask. 'Drink it. I'll be back soon.'

In a daze, Justice watched Matron cross the floor and heard her footsteps descending the wooden stairs. Then she heard a key turn in a lock.

Justice and Dorothy were alone in the tower. They were in a round room, bare except for a single, broken chair. The walls were high, reaching right up to the rafters some twenty feet above. Some bricks were missing at the top and, as

Justice watched, a bat flew in and roosted upside-down on one of the beams. The only light came from the moonlight shining in through these gaps and through the narrow window.

Justice felt her scalp. Yes, there was a lump there, under the hair at the back. She remembered Stella braiding her hair, Rose confronting her in the dormy. Then there was the tower and Dorothy's voice calling to her from the window. Then something, or someone, had hit her on the head.

'What happened?' she said. 'How did I hurt my head?'

'I don't know,' said Dorothy. 'One minute you were talking to me and then you suddenly went quiet. I screamed and screamed and then Matron came. She carried you up the stairs. She's awfully strong. I was petrified. I thought you were dead. But Matron put some stuff under your nose and then you started talking.'

'How did you get locked in here?'

'I told you. I got a note. It said it was from you. It was pushed under my door yesterday morning. The note said that you had a clue and that I should meet you in the tower. When I got here there was no one here but the door was open. I went upstairs and then I heard a key turn in the lock.'

'I saw your signal,' said Justice. 'SOS. Save our souls. So I came to find you.'

'What?' said Dorothy.

'The Morse code signal you gave from the window . . . SOS . . .'

'Morse what?'

A chill ran right through Justice. If Dorothy hadn't sent the signal, then who had? And why – the thought came thundering into her mind, obliterating everything else – why were they still locked in?

'We've got to get out of here,' said Justice.

'Matron's gone to get Miss de Vere,' said Dorothy.

'Miss de Vere might well be the murderer,' said Justice. 'We've got to escape. Hutchins has cleared some of the paths. We could get to the village.'

'I'm scared of Hutchins,' said Dorothy.

'So am I,' said Justice. 'That's why we can't stay here and wait for him.'

She stood up. Her head swam and the room seemed to tilt and sway. Perhaps she did really have concussion. She sat down again and spied the thermos on the stone floor. Maybe some herbal tea would do her good . . .

'Justice!' hissed Dorothy. 'Listen! There are footsteps outside.'

Justice listened. Dorothy was right. Someone was approaching the tower, someone with a stealthy, light tread. She stood up – more gingerly this time – and reached for Dorothy's hand. They heard a key turn in the lock and a voice calling up the stairs. A trembling, blessedly familiar voice.

'Justice? Dorothy?'

It was Stella.

She burst into the room, wearing a coat over her pyjamas and carrying a torch in one hand and a set of keys in the other.

'Stella!' Justice ran over and hugged her. 'How did you get the keys?'

'I took them from Hutchins' cubby hole,' said Stella. 'Matron came into the dormy just after you left and took Rose out with her. When she didn't come back, I thought you must be in danger. I sneaked down and got the keys. Nora and Eva are keeping watch back in the dormy.'

'Why did Matron take Rose out?' said Justice. 'Surely she should have gone to get Miss de Vere?'

There was something there – a pattern, Leslie Light would say – but she still couldn't see it. Suddenly she heard Matron's voice: *All this silliness about notes and secret signals.*

How had Matron known about the notes, in the plural, and the secret signal from the tower? Matron was going to move them to sickbay. Helena had been taken to sickbay too. Before that, Mary had been moved to sickbay when she became delirious after Miss Thomas's visit. What had Dorothy said? *She had a temperature and kept saying this odd thing – that the fog was coming down and she couldn't see.*

'Stella,' said Justice, 'what was the name of the girl who got lost in the fog?'

'What?'

'When we first did games, you told me that Miss Thomas had once lost a girl during a cross-country run when the fog came down. What was her name?'

'Her name was Dilys,' said a voice behind them.

Stella swung round. Matron was standing in the doorway, as calm as ever in her crisply starched uniform.

'Her name was Dilys,' she said, coming into the room and shutting the door behind her. 'And she was my daughter. When the fog came down, two girls went missing – Dilys and Serena, Rose's mother. Miss Thomas went to find them but she only came back with Serena. She left my Dilys out there. They found her the next day. She had fallen into a ditch and died from hypothermia.'

'Is that why you killed Miss Thomas?' said Justice.

'Yes,' said Matron, smiling her orange-gummed smile. 'I always suspected, but I wasn't sure. I wasn't working at the school when Dilys died but, when the Matron's job came up, I applied immediately. I wanted to find out what had really happened. Then, when that maid, Mary, was ill, she was delirious, talking about girls lost in the fog. I remembered that Mary had been sorting out old records and I went through them myself. And I found it. Miss Thomas's report, admitting that after she'd found Serena, she gave up. And left Dilys to die.'

'But why kill Mary? It wasn't her fault,' said Justice, confused.

'Mary?' said Matron, sounding surprised. 'Mary was just a stupid maid. Why on earth would I kill Mary? The girl died of pneumonia.'

'But you *did* kill Miss Thomas?' said Justice. It seemed very important to get this clear.

'Of course I did,' said Matron impatiently. Stella gave a sort of horrified moan and Dorothy began to sob, but Matron continued unperturbed, as if she was telling them a bedtime story.

'I knew that Miss Thomas was blackmailing Miss de Vere – I had seen them sneaking around together after dark. One night I followed and overheard enough to understand.

So it was the easiest thing in the world to get Miss Thomas to meet me by the gymnasium that night, saying I had some information that might be to her advantage. She agreed immediately. Really, she was a most unpleasant person. I watched her setting off through the snow – I thought it might put her off, but no. It was the simplest thing to do to just follow and give her a little *push*.'

Justice frowned. 'What time was that?'

'Oh, I don't know, about eleven maybe? Long after your bedtime,' said Matron.

Well, that explains why there weren't any footprints, thought Justice. There was still a good two hours of snow to come that night. She remembered again watching it fall from the window of Dorothy's room, unaware that someone was lying dead out there.

It also explained why she'd heard Matron talking to Monsieur Pierre by the stairs to the North Turret at around midnight that same night. By that time, Matron had already murdered Miss Thomas. She shivered.

Matron was still talking in that calm, reasonable voice. 'Miss Thomas stopped by the empty pool and I crept up behind her and hit her over the head with a lacrosse stick. I thought it was fitting somehow. Then I pushed her into the pool. That was appropriate too. The times she forced poor

Dilys to swim in there. Serena always got out of swimming *somehow.*'

'Is that why you killed Helena?' said Justice. 'Because you thought she was Rose? To get your revenge on Serena?'

'Very good, yes!' said Matron, smiling, as if Justice had done well in a test. 'I saw her walking along the passage that leads to the attic and I was sure it was Rose. Same long blonde hair, just like her mother. She was wearing her angel costume too. Some angel! Rose and Serena both thought they were the bee's knees. My Dilys was such a pretty girl but no one noticed her next to Serena. Even her own games mistress forgot all about her once she'd saved her *golden girl.*'

'How did you kill Helena?' Justice said, unable to stop her voice trembling.

'I hit her over the head,' said Matron. 'I thought she was Rose because she wasn't wearing her halo.' She sounded quite exasperated. 'Helena was just knocked out. I was going to finish her off with some poison later.' Justice remembered the thermos flask. Thank goodness she hadn't drunk any of the contents.

'Is Helena still alive then?' she said.

'Oh yes,' said Matron. 'She's in sickbay with a sore head. And now I've got to deal with Rose. She won't be swanking around the school much longer.' Matron gave another of those terrifying smiles.

'What have you done with her?' said Justice. 'Why did you take her out of the dormy?'

'Oh my God, you've killed her too, haven't you?' Dorothy started to sob again.

'Not yet,' said Matron. 'I've put her on ice. I'll be back for you three. I'll have those now, Stella, thank you.' She took the keys from Stella and, once more, they heard her footsteps descending the stairs and the tower door being locked behind her.

Justice leapt up and rattled the door as hard as she could. 'We've got to save Rose! Matron's going to kill her.'

Stella came to help, kicking at the wood, punching it. Dorothy joined them, crying with frustration. But the ancient oak was impervious. Their shouts echoed round the stone walls and up into the rafters, sending the bats flying up into the night sky. No one came.

'Rose is going to die,' said Stella, slumping against the wall.

'We can't give up now,' said Justice. 'You've been wonderful, Stella . . . getting Hutchins's keys, rescuing us. We've *got* to find a way of raising the alarm. If we stay here,

Matron will kill Rose for sure. And then she'll come back for us.'

'Matron saw us in the North Turret that night,' said Dorothy. 'She must have thought we knew that she'd tried to kill Helena.'

'That's why she lured you here,' said Justice, thinking it all through. Matron must have devised a plan to get the two of them out of the way, a plan that played on Justice's love of adventures, secret notes and clues. Justice ground her teeth with frustration. How could she have let Matron trick her like that? They couldn't let her get away with it.

'Nora and Eva are waiting in the dormy,' she said. 'What will they do when you don't come back?'

'They'll go for Miss de Vere, I suppose,' said Stella, still sitting on the ground, looking defeated.

'If Matron doesn't get to them first,' said Dorothy.

Stella gave a moan. 'She's going to kill all of us.'

'Not if I have anything to do with it,' said Justice. 'Now what's the time? Does anyone have a watch?'

But Justice and Stella were in their nightclothes and Dorothy didn't own a watch. Justice went to the window. It was still dark outside but she thought she could see some glimmers of light over the marshes. Dawn was on its way.

'The windows are too narrow to climb through,' she said. 'Let's try shouting.'

They all yelled 'Help!' as loudly as they could but their voices just echoed uselessly against the stone walls.

'It's no good,' said Stella. 'No one's there. It's the middle of the night.'

'We have to try,' said Justice, but the strain of shouting had made her head buzz unpleasantly, and she put a hand to the wall to steady herself.

Then she heard something. She almost felt it vibrating through the stone.

Footsteps crunching through the snow, coming towards the tower.

'It's Matron!' Dorothy grabbed Justice's arm.

'No,' said Justice, listening intently. 'The tread is too heavy. It's a man.'

Then they heard a deep voice calling. 'Is anyone there?'

It was Hutchins. The three girls all ran to the window and began shouting at once.

'We were locked in!'

'It was Matron!'

'Rose is in danger!'

The handyman stood by the door, dark against the snow. He had a lantern in one hand and a spade in the other.

'What's going on?' he shouted up at them. 'Someone stole my keys.'

'That was me,' said Stella. 'I knew Justice and Dorothy were trapped here and I had to rescue them somehow. Please believe us . . .'

Justice looked down at the handyman. She remembered how he'd shovelled through the snow to find Miss Thomas's body. He'd seemed shocked then. Surely he wasn't in league with Matron? They had no hope but to trust him.

'Please,' she said. 'Matron locked us in. She killed Miss Thomas. She told us so. And we think she's got Rose somewhere.'

'Matron . . .' Hutchins seemed to be turning the idea over in his head. Justice was almost jumping up and down with impatience.

'That's why she made you clear the path to the tower,' she said. 'It was so that she could lock us in here.'

'She made me clear the path to the ice house too,' said Hutchins.

'The ice house!' Justice turned to Stella and Dorothy with horrified eyes. 'Matron said she was keeping Rose on ice. She must want her to die of hypothermia, like Dilys. Rose is locked in the ice house. We have to get to her!'

'But how can he let us out?' said Dorothy. 'Matron's got his keys.'

Then they saw the handyman reach into his pocket and hold up something that glimmered in the light of his lantern. 'Lucky I've got these then . . .'

A moment later, they were following the handyman across the snow, back through the wood towards the outhouses. Dawn was breaking now, shafts of light shining through the trees, the birds singing around them. *Please God*, Justice prayed, *don't let us be too late.*

The three girls held hands as they ran. The snow was melting but the ground was still icy in places. Several times one of them almost fell but the others kept her upright. Hutchins marched ahead, a dark shape in the hazy light. Where was Matron now? wondered Justice. Had she locked Eva and Nora in the dormy? Had she drugged them to make them sleep or done something even worse? And what about Rose? Justice imagined Rose locked in the freezing ice house, too cold and terrified to scream. Beautiful, annoying, superior Rose. *Please let them be in time to save her.*

Eventually they reached the windowless, sinister building, standing on its own beyond the kitchen garden.

'Rose!' yelled Justice as soon as they were near. 'Rose! Are you there?'

They all stood still listening. Hutchins fumbled for his keys and, from the ice house, there came the faintest sound, like a kitten mewing.

'Open the door,' begged Justice. 'Please!'

'Not so fast,' said another voice.

Matron was standing behind them.

'Go back to the house, Hutchins,' she said, with all the authority of a teacher and a nurse. 'I'll deal with these girls.'

Justice turned to the handyman who was looking at Matron in a strange, fixed way. Surely he wouldn't listen to her? He seemed to be hesitating. Justice remembered how Hutchins had offered her his flask on the day that they had tunnelled through the snow. He'd seemed to quite like her then. Her head was feeling funny again and there were black dots in front of her eyes, dancing on the snow. Black on white. 'Please!' She was crying now.

'Please,' Dorothy added. 'Rose is locked in there. She's freezing to death.'

Hutchins had turned to look at Justice. Very slowly, not taking his eyes off her, he took out his key fob. Then several things happened at once. A voice shouted 'Wait!' and Justice turned to see several figures hurrying towards them. One looked familiar. So dear and familiar that she started to cry out. And then, to her eternal shame, she fainted.

CHAPTER 22

It was just like before. Rising out of blackness, the lights, the shapes, the voices. Only this time she opened her eyes to see her father sitting on the end of her bed.

'Hallo, Justice.'

'Dad!' She struggled to sit up.

'Don't get up.' Dad gently pushed her back on her pillows. 'I think you've got concussion. The doctor will be here soon.'

'How did you get here?'

'I drove down as soon as I got the message. The roads are starting to clear now.'

'But who sent you the message? You couldn't have got my letter. The telephone lines are down and there's no post.'

'I did,' said another voice. Justice hadn't noticed Miss de Vere standing in the shadows of the dormy.

And suddenly Justice realised what the boxes were for, the ones marked 'electrical equipment'. 'You were trying to send radio messages!' said Justice. 'That's what the equipment was for. I saw the boxes in the storeroom below the North Turret and you and Monsieur Pierre carrying them down into the basement. Dorothy said she heard voices coming from the North Turret. You must have been trying to find the right place to broadcast from. That's why you were both there that night, the night Miss Thomas was killed.'

'Goodness, Justice,' said Dad. 'You have been busy.'

'Your daughter is an incorrigible sleuth,' said Miss de Vere.

'Thank you,' said Dad, though Justice wasn't sure if it was meant as a compliment. 'Yes,' he turned to Justice. 'When Dolores . . . Miss de Vere finally got through to me, I came at once. And I brought a Scotland Yard detective with me.'

'Really?' Justice sat up again. 'Can I meet him?'

'Later,' said Dad. 'He's not quite what you'd expect. At present he has Evelyn Webb in custody.'

'Evelyn Webb? Oh, Matron. I didn't suspect her at first because she seemed so horrible. I thought a murderer would be more charming. That's why I thought it was you,' she said to Miss de Vere.

'Thank you,' said the headmistress politely.

'But then I put it together. The link had to be Mary. When she was in sickbay she was talking about fog and I remembered something Stella said – just a casual remark – about the girl who got lost in the fog.'

'No remarks are ever casual,' said Herbert Jones QC.

'I should have paid more attention when Rose mentioned Matron's daughter. But Rose was so sure that Matron adored her. And her mother too.'

'I think Matron was quite fond of Rose at first,' said Miss de Vere. 'She didn't even bear any ill-will towards Serena until she saw the report about the cross-country run and decided that Miss Thomas had not searched long enough.'

'Miss Thomas was blackmailing you, wasn't she?' said Justice. 'That was why you were going out to the tower at night.'

'Yes, she was,' said Miss de Vere. 'I'll leave it to your father to explain why. I need to get back to my school. I fear tongues may be wagging.'

That was underestimating things in Justice's opinion. She thought that tongues would have broken loose from their moorings and be wandering around the school on their own by now.

When the headmistress had gone she was surprised when her dad caught her in a fierce hug.

'Justice, I've been so worried about you.'

'Why?' Justice wriggled free. 'I can look after myself.'

'You certainly can,' said Dad. 'Though it sounds like you've had able assistants in Dorothy and Stella. You've made friends here.'

Justice thought about sitting curled up on Dorothy's bed, of Stella running through the snow to save them, of Eva and Nora saying that they'd be sorry if she left. Even Rose had moved away from the door that night to let her pass. She remembered snowballs and ghost stories and midnight feasts, and in spite of herself, she found herself smiling. 'I suppose I have,' she said. 'Not sure about the teachers though.'

'On the contrary,' said Dad. 'Miss de Vere likes you a lot. She didn't even seem annoyed that you had originally cast her as the villain of the piece.' He was smiling now.

'What about Rose?' said Justice. 'Will she be all right?'

'I think so. She was very cold, of course, but Miss de Vere wrapped her in blankets and took her to the teachers' common room. Apparently that's the only warm place in the school.'

'That's true,' said Justice.

'You saved Rose,' said Dad. 'She'll be your friend for life.'

'I doubt it,' said Justice. Then she remembered what she really wanted to know. 'Why was Miss Thomas blackmailing Miss de Vere? Was it because she'd found out that she murdered her husband?'

Justice had never thought that her father could be lost for words but now he just stared at her, his mouth slightly open in a way he had once described as 'uncouth'.

'How did you . . .' he eventually managed.

'I saw the envelope that the blackmail letter was in, addressed to Mrs Guy Goddard,' explained Justice, 'and a little while later I remembered that case of yours. It was a murder trial. *Rex v Goddard*. A wife accused of murdering her husband.'

'You remembered my case . . .' repeated her father. 'I didn't know you were interested in the law. I thought it was all detective stories with you.'

'Of course I'm interested in your cases,' said Justice. 'I'm your daughter. And besides, I'm a girl called Justice. What else would I be interested in?'

Herbert Jones QC smiled and shook his head in amazement.

'So, did Miss de Vere murder her husband?' asked Justice.

Her father seemed to pull himself together. 'No. She didn't kill him. She was found innocent and she *was* innocent. Guy Goddard was a brute who drank a lot and treated his wife extremely badly. He fell down some stairs when he was drunk. Miss de Vere had nothing to do with it. The jury acquitted her unanimously.'

'But Miss Thomas was still blackmailing her.'

'Yes, even though Miss de Vere was innocent, parents wouldn't want their daughters going to a school where the headmistress had been accused of murder. That's why Dolores went back to her maiden name.'

'But *you* didn't mind sending me here,' said Justice.

Herbert smiled. 'I think Miss de Vere is a very singular woman. I thought you'd get on.'

Justice thought of Miss de Vere warning her about boarding school, about the way that she could seem charming one minute and terrifying the next, the expression on her face when Justice had challenged her.

'Miss de Vere is pretty scary sometimes,' she said.

'All the best people are,' said Dad. 'I hope I terrify the prosecution in court. And you can be pretty formidable yourself, Justice.'

'Can I?' said Justice, pleased.

'Yes, you can,' said Herbert. 'You're a very clever girl, Justice, and you can learn a lot from Miss de Vere. She's a brilliant scholar. Just as your mother was.' He looked sad for a moment and Justice decided to change the subject.

'I thought perhaps Miss de Vere was in love with Monsieur Pierre,' said Justice. 'I always seemed to see them together.'

'No, he was just helping her get the radio working in case they got snowed in again, and a lucky thing too,' said Herbert. 'From what I understand, it was a sixth-form student who was infatuated with the French master.'

'Helena Bliss?' said Justice. 'Was that why she was always sneaking around at night? Of course, she must have known that Miss de Vere and Monsieur Pierre used to meet in the North Turret to use the radio equipment. That's why I saw her in there that night and the other time . . . the time when Matron tried to kill her.'

'Yes,' said Herbert. 'It seems that Helena was in the wrong place at the wrong time.'

'Is she all right now?' said Justice.

'Apparently so,' said Herbert. 'The doctor has examined her and she's suffering from nothing more than a severe headache.'

So Helena Bliss would soon be prancing around the school in her halo again. The thought made Justice feels strangely contented.

'Did Miss de Vere know that Matron attacked Helena?' she said.

'No,' said Dad. 'It seemed that Dolores . . . Miss de Vere . . . trusted Matron completely. That's why she left Helena in her care.'

'We all trusted Matron,' said Justice. 'She was horrible, but we trusted her. What's going to happen now?'

'The police will investigate,' said Herbert, 'and Evelyn Webb – Matron – will go to trial, unless it can be proved that the balance of her mind is disturbed. I just hope that the school can survive this scandal.'

'Oh, it'll be forgotten in a week,' said Justice. 'All people here care about is whether the teachers dye their hair or what there's going to be for supper.'

It wasn't forgotten in a week but, by the end of term, people had found other things to talk about. There was a Christmas lunch with crackers and something purporting to be turkey. There were carols in the church with Miss Evans wheezing away on the organ, several seconds behind the singers. They even put on the nativity play with Helena playing the part of the Angel Gabriel. Rose, seemingly recovered from her experience in the ice house, also played her part with aplomb. Justice was word-perfect as the narrator and Stella as Mary managed to look fairly happy when told that she was about to marry Joseph (Pamela Powers) and travel to Bethlehem to be counted.

It was rumoured that some girls wouldn't be coming back after Christmas but, for the most part, the last morning of term was taken up with swapping addresses and tearful promises to keep in touch.

'They'll be seeing each other in four weeks,' Justice said to Stella as they passed two weeping friends in the hall.

'Four weeks is a long time,' said Stella. 'A whole month! You must write to me every day, Justice, or I'll go into a decline.'

They both laughed but there was a slight constraint between them. Justice's father had told her that, if it was what she wanted, she could leave Highbury House and go to a day school in London. 'I've seen how well you can look after yourself,' he said. 'I don't need to worry about you coming home to an empty house if I'm working late. And after everything that's gone on, you'll probably never want to see Highbury House again, I imagine?'

Part of Justice agreed with him. She thought of how much she'd wanted to hear him say that she could leave, that she could come home again, that he trusted her. She thought of finding Helena's body, of waking in the tower to see Matron bending over her, her terrible smile. She would be happy never to think about any of that ever again. But, on the other hand, there was Dorothy, a true friend. And Stella, who had come to rescue her in the tower. And Eva and Nora and all the rest of the girls really. Even Rose, whose attitude towards Justice had not softened when she found out that Justice had saved her life. Justice rather admired her for that.

In the dormy the Barnowls were packing their trunks.

'I'm going to a New Year's Eve ball,' Rose was saying. 'I'm going to wear a long dress, silver with sparkles, and Mummy says I can wear my hair up.'

'Up what?' said Justice, coming into the room.

Rose threw her a withering look. 'You wouldn't understand. You'll probably spend the whole hols *reading*.'

That was, in fact, pretty much what Justice had planned. She and Dad were going to have a quiet Christmas; reading, going for walks in the park, listening to the wireless. They were having Christmas Day with Peter and his parents, and she might be able to meet up with Stella as she lived in London, but otherwise they were going to be on their own in the house and Justice realised that she was looking forward to it. She had decided she was going to reread all Mum's Leslie Light books again. Meeting a real detective, Inspector Porlock of the Yard, had slightly changed her view of the police. They were always portrayed as rather stupid in crime novels – it was the amateur detective who always solved the murder – but Porlock seemed to know exactly what was going on, the undercurrents below as well as what was on the surface. He was a small man with deceptively mild blue eyes but he missed nothing.

'Evelyn Webb must have come to dislike all schoolgirls,' he said to Justice, 'and schoolgirl friendships in particular.' Justice remembered Matron warning her against getting too close to Stella. *It's not always a good thing to have just one particular friend. They might let you down when you most need them.* Matron must have felt that both Serena and Miss Thomas had let Dilys down. Justice might even have felt quite sorry for her if she hadn't tried to kill Justice and her friends.

Inspector Porlock had also praised Justice's detective work. 'Smart thinking about the footsteps in the snow,' he said. 'Looks like you've got a gift for this sort of thing.'

Maybe she was a detective after all. Justice pondered these words as she watched the Barnowls throwing clothes, books and the occasional piece of uneaten tuck into their trunks.

'I hear you won't be coming back after Christmas, Justice,' said Rose, interrupting her thoughts. She always seemed to know everyone's secrets. 'You're going to some potty day school.'

'Oh, please stay with us, Justice,' said Eva. 'We play rounders in the spring. It's super.'

Provided the new games mistress doesn't turn out to be another tyrant who loses her pupils in the fog, thought Justice. She looked at the faces in front of her. Eva hopeful. Nora encouraging. Rose scornful. Stella trying not to show how much she cared.

'I suppose I'll stay,' she said at last, with a slight smile. 'The next term can hardly be worse, after all.'

Don't miss ...

A GIRL CALLED JUSTICE

on her next case

COMING SOON!

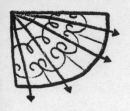
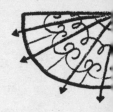

Acknowledgements

Highbury House Boarding School for the Daughters of Gentlefolk is entirely fictional. It is, however, loosely based on Heath House in Weybridge, the school attended by my mother, Sheila, in the 1930s. Like Justice, Sheila was brought up by her father (though he was an actor not a lawyer) and she too heartily disliked boarding school. She missed her father and Matron told her off for talking about him too much. Sheila consoled herself by breaking as many school rules as she could and by reading detective novels. She also wrote some very exciting adventure stories which often featured a schoolgirl heroine. Mum died in 2014 but, in every sense, this is her book.

Many thanks to my editors at Hachette Children's Group, Sarah Lambert and Katherine Agar. Thanks to Kate for her wonderfully helpful notes and for entering so fully into Justice's adventures. Thanks as ever to my wonderful agent, Rebecca Carter, and to Quercus Books who publish my adult fiction.

Love and thanks always to my husband, Andrew, and to our children, Alex and Juliet, who have helped me come up with so many murder plots. Though you are not, strictly speaking, children any more, Alex and Juliet – this is for you.

EG
2019

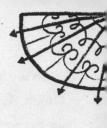